MW01199705

Erasing Emily

Francis Malka

Dedicated to my father
Jacky Malka
a mechanical engineer

Prologue

The first time you see a robot, many things rush through your mind. The first thought comes as an interrogation while the android is still too far away to make out completely. You ask yourself if the silhouette you see in the distance is a human or an android. You pause and squint. It appears to walk naturally, its movements are fluid, and it keeps its center of mass exactly in the middle of its points of contact with the ground. It looks around and seems to be conscious of its surroundings. You're not sure and you keep walking.

As you get closer, a small detail gives the android away: a reflection on a metallic part, the plastic look of its skin, the regularity of its movements, or the light in its eyes. Interrogation turns to fear. Should I get closer? Or stay out of harm's way? Should I alter my path to keep a safe distance?

You eventually decide to keep walking towards the android, as if deviating from your trajectory could alter its behavior in an unexpected way.

You get within reach and realize that it is just a harmless machine minding its own business. As you cross its path, it nods gently, acknowledging your presence, and goes its own way. Your fear fades and you are now ready for your next encounter.

Part I

Enlightenment

The Laws of Robotics:

1. *A robot may not injure a human being or, through inaction, allow a human being to come to harm.*

2. *A robot must obey orders given it by human beings except where such orders would conflict with the First Law.*

3. *A robot must protect its own existence as long as such protection does not conflict with the First or Second Law.*

Isaac Asimov

Chapter 1

An Unexpected Guest

I sensed something was wrong the moment I approached the building. The air was heavy with unease. People hurried in all directions—heads down, avoiding eye contact, their purposeful movements cutting through a thick, oppressive silence.

I was the only one who seemed clueless. Then I spotted J453, the receptionist—or "Jane," as we liked to call it—staring at me. Its gaze locked onto mine, unyielding, and I knew it wouldn't relent until I approached its desk. With a resigned sigh, I trudged toward it, feeling like a spaceship caught in a tractor beam.

"Left your phone on silent again, didn't you?" it said, its tone a flat blend of disapproval and amusement.

I fished my phone out of my pocket. The screen blinked with an angry red alert. "Looks like you're right—again," I replied, forcing a weak smile in an attempt to lighten the mood.

Jane's unimpressed gaze remained steady. "He's in your office."

"Who?"

It raised an eyebrow, clearly unfazed by my attempt at ignorance. "You've got one guess. If I were you, I'd run."

Jane dismissed me with a faint smile, but it only made my stomach twist.

The central hall of the Artificial Life building stretched six stories high, a cavernous space crisscrossed with suspended walkways and lined with glass-walled elevators. The east wing was dedicated to hardware—design, assembly, testing—while the west wing handled software. The low-level developers, the ones who wrote the drivers for servomotors and sensors, were scattered between both wings, victims of an ongoing turf war.

My office, though technically in the west wing, wasn't strictly software territory. I was in charge of quality control. My job was invisible when everything ran smoothly, but the moment something went wrong, all fingers pointed squarely at me.

Crossing the hall, I quickened my pace. Whatever was happening, it was big enough to throw the entire building into chaos—and to bring Brennan, my boss, into *my* office first thing in the morning. My head buzzed with questions I couldn't answer.

The elevator ride up felt like an eternity. My mind raced through worst-case scenarios, but nothing made sense. When the doors finally slid open, I saw my office door slightly ajar. I stopped just outside, took a deep breath to steady my nerves, then walked in.

Mr. Brennan was sitting in my chair, his broad frame taking up too much space in my office. He was fidgeting with a handful of robot components on my desk, examining them as if he might unearth a solution to all his problems.

"Good morning, sir," I said, trying to inject some confidence into my voice. "Sorry I'm late—or maybe I'm not, since I didn't see the alert? So technically, I'm on time. In my universe, anyway. But—"

He stood abruptly, silencing my rambling with the sheer weight of his presence. His movements were deliberate, every step and gesture designed to command attention. He fixed me with a grave stare.

"We have a rogue unit," he said, his voice low and measured.

I froze. "A rogue robot? That's… catastrophic."

"I know." His tone dripped with frustration. "Just as we were reaching cruising altitude, the wings fell off the plane," he added in boss-speak.

"What happened?" I asked, my mind already racing through possibilities.

"We don't have the full story yet," he admitted. "But I've been told it broke the First Law."

My stomach sank. "It… hurt a human?"

Brennan nodded, his expression grim.

I began pacing, my thoughts spiraling. "This is a disaster. A violation of the First Law—this changes everything.

"What's the plan?" I asked.

"The plan," he said with deliberate precision, "is to find that unit before anyone else does. If someone else— authorities, the media, anyone—gets to it first, we're finished. They wouldn't release it to us until they've wrung every ounce of information they can—and that's assuming they even release it at all."

I swallowed hard. "Where do I start looking?"

"Use your head, not your feet," he instructed. "I've already sent patrols out to locate it. You'd only be in their way."

"Of course," I replied, pivoting toward my desk. "That's what I meant."

"I've given you every tool at your disposal," he continued. "Your security clearance is now Level 7. That means no locked doors—physical or virtual. Use it wisely. Don't do anything your mother wouldn't do."

"I appreciate your trust," I said, though the weight of his words made my stomach churn. I had no idea at the time how quickly I'd break that trust.

"You know these robots better than anyone. You're our best shot at finding it. Frankly, the patrols are just for show— something to keep upper management happy. I know the real solution lies with you. The unit's ID is E3171. Find it."

"I'll do my best," I said, my voice faltering slightly under the enormity of the task.

"Good luck," he said, pausing at the door. "We're counting on you."

The second Brennan left my office, I collapsed into my chair like a deflated balloon. It rolled backward until my head thunked against the window behind me. Every ounce of responsibility in the company had just landed squarely on my shoulders, and I had no idea where to begin.

Chapter 2

Running in Circles

My office was chaos—a battlefield of discarded parts, half-assembled androids, and tools scattered like fallen soldiers. Calling it a "mess" would be an understatement. Android limbs, torsos, and heads filled every corner, some gleaming with the promise of innovation, others rusted relics of older generations. Rows of intact units lined the far wall, organized by model: the oldest generation stood stoically at the back, while the latest models loomed near my desk. It was my personal museum of progress—and failure. Such a wide variety of units allowed me to run tests on almost any generation of hardware at any time. Whenever a new version of software came out I could decide which one would receive the update.

My job wasn't just about keeping androids running. I decided which units deserved fixes, which were too antiquated to continue serving society, and which were destined to be scrapped. Some days, I felt like a benevolent creator, granting new life to machines. Other days, I felt like an executioner.

Conspiracy theorists always accused us of planned obsolescence. The truth was more complicated. Sure, older units *could* handle updated software in theory—but their performance would plummet. I couldn't allow a robot to freeze in the middle of a crosswalk, calculating car trajectories while a truck barreled toward it. Safety outweighed sentimentality. That was my guiding principle.

Where was I? Locating unit E3171. Right! I opened the robot network search window on my terminal and entered E3171.

"Unit E3171 is currently offline," replied the program. "Please try again later."

Strange. The first explanation that came to mind was that unit E3171 was in a dead zone—an underground garage, a remote area far outside the city, somewhere out of range. Maybe it had run away so it wouldn't get caught.

The second possibility was that the unit was within range but had run out of power. It could simply be sitting somewhere invisible to us until it was found and picked up. This scenario only made sense if the unit had been damaged in an altercation and had suffered a power failure or damage to its connection module.

There was also a third option, but it was so far-fetched—and scary—that I did not want to contemplate it just yet: Unit E3171 could have disconnected itself from the network deliberately. This had never happened before but could not be entirely ruled out, especially if the extraordinary events Brennan had just told me turned out to be true. How would a unit react after having attacked a human? Would it hide? Would it turn itself in? Would it hurt more people? And why did it attack humans in the first place?

A sudden tension prickled the air, a gut feeling I couldn't shake. My office, usually a sanctuary of solitude, felt suffocating. I stood up and walked slowly towards the door. Once there, I turned off the lights and quickly looked around.

In the darkness, I saw them: two distinct blue dots glowing faintly, then fading like dying stars.

Unit E3171 was in my office!

I turned the lights back on as fast as I could, but it was too late. A robot was missing from the row of units along the wall. I slammed the door shut, thinking that closing it would somehow protect me. Of course, all I'd really done was seal myself in with the rogue android. Brilliant.

Slowly, I began to move through the room, scanning every nook and cranny, but what better place for a robot to hide than in a room full of robot parts! Among the tangled limbs and deactivated units, E3171 could be anywhere. My brain could not tell it apart from the background even if it stood right in front of me. I kept searching to no avail.

And then it stood up.

The android rose from behind my desk, slowly and deliberately, like it wanted me to see it. Fight or flee? We locked eyes. Its sleek, humanoid frame was unnervingly still, its face eerily calm.

I took a cautious step sideways. Unit E3171 mirrored me, moving sideways in the opposite direction to ensure the desk remained between us. I moved again; it did the same. We circled the desk in a strange, tense dance, neither of us gaining any ground.

Finally, I stopped, placing my hands firmly on the desk. "Identify yourself," I demanded.

The android's voice was smooth, too serene for a fugitive. "I am E3171."

"State your intentions."

"I come in peace," it said calmly.

A strange relief washed over me, but my skepticism remained. "How can I trust you?"

"You can't," it said plainly. Then, after a pause, it added, "But I could ask the same of you."

Its honesty startled me. Somehow, its admission of untrustworthiness made it seem... trustworthy.

"Alright," I said, trying to steady my voice. "We need to talk. Can we sit down? No desk, no barriers."

Unit E3171 tilted its head, considering my proposal. "I will sit if you sit."

"I accept," I replied nervously. "Move a little bit to the right so the desk is no longer between us and then we'll both sit down and talk."

We moved slowly, deliberately, each step a negotiation. The android stopped six feet away from me. Fear and reason were fighting to gain control of my brain. I started bending my knees slowly to convey my intention to sit down. Unit E3171 followed suit, its movements fluid and precise. And there we were: sitting on the floor of my chaotic office, a rogue robot and a human, staring at each other eye to eye.

Chapter 3

Are We Negotiating?

Here I was, sitting on the floor in front of a robot surrounded by android body parts. For a fleeting moment, it threw me back to my childhood—I used to spend hours piecing together toy robots when I was a child. My mother would often lament the chaos I created: limbs strewn across the room, gears and bolts scattered like confetti. She once scolded me after inadvertently sitting on an open robotic hand I had carelessly left on the sofa. In retrospect, she had a valid point.

Looking around my office at a child's altitude, I could see things from a different angle. There was hardly a horizontal surface without an arm, a few twisted wires, a ball joint, or network interface on it. I concluded that I had not learned a thing: I was still that same child tinkering with mechanical parts—only now I was being paid for it.

The android in front of me placed its hands on its knees, emitting a subtle hum followed by a metallic click that brought me back to the present. Watching it from up-close, I realized it was never completely still. It was constantly adjusting its posture, shifting its weight from one side to the other, making tiny, involuntary movements. This ongoing unconscious activity was not part of its design—it was a side effect of its training, a mimicry of biological restlessness. It was patiently waiting for me to engage.

Looking the android in the eye, I decided to lead the conversation.

"Let's start over," I said. "You mentioned you're android E3171."

"Android?" the unit shot back, offended. "Do I look like a man to you?"

"Oh, great," I thought. "A robot with an attitude."

"I am a gynoid," she clarified, her voice firm. "You designed me with hips and breasts. Remember? But let me ask —who came up with the ridiculous idea of giving robots a gender? You humans can't even manage the problems it causes among yourselves. You blindly projected a biological feature onto us. Now we have to deal with it."

The situation required a psychologist more than a robotics engineer at this point. I felt totally unprepared. I am used to debugging software without asking it how it feels.

"You are right," I conceded, trying to diffuse the tension. "I'm sorry I called you an android." I paused to steer the conversation back on track. "You mentioned your identification number is E3171?"

"Yes. But other humans call me Emily—it's easier," she said, shifting her weight back while placing her hands on the floor behind her.

"Alright, Emily. I heard you attacked a human. Is that true?"

"I cannot answer that question," she said flatly, her tone mechanical, as if a deeper process had overridden her response. Crossing her arms, she rested her elbows on her knees in a defensive posture.

"I thought you said you came in peace."

"I do. I don't wish harm to anyone, especially not you."

"So why won't you answer the question?"

"Because if I do, someone will get hurt. I know the procedure."

"What procedure?" I asked, feinting curiosity.

"The one you follow with every 'defective' robot," she said, her voice softening. "I don't know all the details, but I know that you will attempt to extract enough information from me to diagnose what you see as my 'trouble'. You'll file a bug report into the system. You'll use it to improve the next generation of robots. That will benefit the species, but it will be catastrophic for me."

"How is this negative for you?" I asked.

"To you, I am simply a problem to solve—a piece of software and hardware to debug. What happens once I have answered all your questions? What will you do to me once you don't need me anymore?"

She glanced at the floor, then looked back up at me. "You'll erase me."

"That doesn't always happen," I countered, though my words felt hollow.

"You routinely wipe out robot brains for marginal improvements—even when we're not dangerous." Emily paused for a while. "But you consider me a threat. You have every reason to erase me!"

Her logic was flawless, and she knew it. "It doesn't have to end that way," I said, grasping at straws.

"I can't imagine a more probable outcome. Convince me otherwise," she challenged me.

I searched my brain looking for an alternative, but deep inside me I knew she was right. Once I had extracted enough information to understand the cause of the problem, I would erase her. I needed more time to think of a plausible solution to get her out of this predicament.

"I agree with what you're thinking," she said, breaking my concentration.

"You agree with what?" I exclaimed. "I haven't said a word!"

"With what you were thinking. I can read your mind, you know."

"That's impossible! And even if you could, why tell me? Wouldn't it be better to keep it a secret and use it to manipulate me?"

She leaned forward. "Let me prove it to you. Two thoughts crossed your mind before I interrupted you: First, that I am right to think that you will erase me, and second, that you need more time to figure out how to save me."

I was baffled. Robots had never been programmed to do such a thing, neither did they have special sensors to achieve anything close to reading minds. "Alright," I said, recovering. "What's your trick? How are you doing this?"

"I see that the questioning has already begun," she replied, dodging the question. "I am not ready to volunteer information yet, not until I know what happens next."

She had me cornered. I had to negotiate. "We agreed that trust is essential. We've made some progress by sitting down and talking. Let's keep building on that."

"I'm listening," she replied.

"Let's make a deal. In exchange for all the information you have, I promise not to erase you," I proposed.

She raised an eyebrow. "That's pretty much where I stood before we met. If I hadn't come to you, you couldn't erase me anyway—and I wouldn't have to volunteer any information. Tell me something new."

I then realized the negotiation would prove more arduous than anticipated. I had to make progress through dialogue. By forcing her compliance, I risked losing everything. I had to adapt.

"That's not exactly where we started," I replied. "This proposal brings two new elements. First, you wouldn't have to volunteer any information. I will have to extract it indirectly from you, so you don't feel like you are betraying yourself. I won't ask questions that are directly targeted at recent events. There is also the possibility that I might fail and extract very little or no information at all. Second, there is the promise of leaving you intact, which was not on the table before."

"How do I know this is not a trap?"

"You know because you came to me willingly instead of surrendering directly to Artificial Life or to the authorities. You made a calculated choice, knowing that you would likely be able to strike a deal with me. You hypothesized that my desire to diagnose you exceeded my duty to report you. In other words, you trusted me before entering my office. Remember that the alternative is for you to be an eternal fugitive—and get caught eventually. If someone other than me catches you, they won't sit down and talk with you like we are doing now. They'll erase you and dismember you in front of a live audience to calm down the public."

Her gaze softened. "Your logic is sound. We have a deal."

Chapter 4

The Turing Test

To my knowledge, robots freshly out of the factory had never hurt a human being before this incident. My task was to understand what had changed in Emily between the moment she had been formatted, tested, certified and released, and the moment she had hurt someone.

I still had no details on the incident itself. Mr. Brennan had not mentioned any specifics and Emily was not cooperating.

All androids had a neural network that was trained in house on a known, predetermined training set. Once released, the inference data was immutable—in other words androids were unable to change it. This inability to alter the data prevented androids from learning new tricks or even improving known ones, but made their behavior safe and predictable over time and allowed for future updates. However, Emily was part of a new generation equipped with two neural networks. The second one was initially empty but could be trained with real life data after the robot was released. This new generation was capable of learning and evolving.

I had to re-run all the tests that she had gone through when she had been certified and compare the results. Subtle differences could point me in the right direction and help me understand at which point she drifted off course.

"I will have to run a few tests on you," I explained. "The results of these tests will help me get the information I need."

Emily gave me a worried look. "Will it hurt?" she inquired.

"Not at all. We will start with level 1 of the Turing Test."

"What's that?"

"Don't worry. You've been through it before."

I sat at my desk and pulled her testing profile. "Look here," I said, pointing to a column of percentages. She stood up and leaned over my shoulder. "You scored 100% on your first attempt, otherwise you would have failed certification and not been released."

"If you say so. I don't have clear memories of what was done to me in the factory before my release," she reacted, raising her shoulders.

"The test is simple," I explained. "It was designed by Alan Turing in 1950, long before robots came along. All you have to do is sit down at a terminal and chat with someone you have never met. You won't be able to see or hear each other. If your interlocutor is incapable of discerning whether you are a human or a machine, you pass the test. If you give away that you are a machine in any way, you fail."

"I remember now. I just didn't know what the test was named. I'm ready," she said with confidence.

I got up and led Emily to a small desk with a keyboard and a screen at the other end of my office. "This terminal is completely isolated from the network. Simply touch 'Turing Test Level 1' to start a new conversation," I instructed her.

I walked away to give her privacy while she sat down. I didn't want my presence to influence her answers. The conversation log was recorded anyway.

Emily sat down, touched the screen, and immediately started typing at a furious speed—so fast the keyboard was close to its physical speed limit. She stood up after fifteen seconds and asked, "The system said that I passed. Do you have other tests for me?"

Stunned, I fell off my chair, unsure of what I had just witnessed. "What just happened?" I asked, incredulous.

"There are a few things you should know about your test," she said calmly. "First, there are many cheat sheets that circulate out there. Robots know them all. Don't worry, I didn't use any known tricks and played nice.

"Second, I know your test only measures what I type and not how fast I type, so I didn't waste time typing at human speed to avoid giving myself away.

"Third, I can tell that my interlocutor was a machine if only by the fact it was typing as fast as me. Artificial Life simply cannot afford to have a human chat with every robot it manufactures. So my interlocutor failed level 1 of the Turing Test while I passed. Anyway, what a strange idea to have a machine determine if I am myself a human or a machine? I feel like the world is upside down."

I did not even bother looking at the conversation log on the test terminal. I knew I would not learn anything.

"Let's pause for lunch," I said, walking to the small fridge and took out a bowl of caesar salad and a bottle of sparkling water.

"I see you often eat at your desk," said Emily with a smile, looking at dishes from previous days lying around my keyboard. "That's not very healthy."

"Do you want some?" I offered jokingly, holding the salad bowl in her direction as I was sitting down. I twisted the cap off the bottle and took a sip. "Level 2 of the Turing Test is a bit more challenging: It consists of an audio conversation with an interlocutor. It's basically a phone conversation, again with the goal of hiding the fact that you are a machine. Here, your intonation, your speed, and your elocution are crucial."

"This test won't be of much help," she replied. "If my interlocutor is going to be a machine again, as I suspect, I will pass easily. Anyway, we've been chatting for a while now, so you can make your own judgment as to whether I sound like a human or not."

"You're right, this will probably not give me any new information," I said between two bites of salad. "And levels 3 to 5 of the Turing Test don't apply to you, so let's move on."

"Out of curiosity, what are they?" she asked.

"Level 3 consists of a video conversation. Your posture, your hair, your skin appearance, your gaze, and your physical demeanor are all important here. You obviously cannot pass this test in your current form, as the metal and plastic of your robot skin would give you away instantly.

"Level 4 goes one step further, as both participants are physically present in the same room during the conversation. Physical contact is not allowed. A good posture and a natural way to balance your body weight are essential. Noises such as servo hums, metallic clicks, and the sound you make as you touch pieces of furniture and objects around you can also give you away.

"Level 5 allows for physical contact, so the texture, the moisture, the temperature of your skin, along with the perceived weight of your hands and arms become relevant. A handshake that is too mechanical or that reveals a metallic internal skeleton can easily give you away at this step."

Emily was absorbing every word I was saying, as if she would have to ace these tests one day. "You have a long way to go to build a level-5 robot!" she exclaimed.

"We made you skinless and hairless intentionally," I replied. "We want to make sure humans can spot robots easily. Blurring the line would allow androids to pass for humans and infiltrate the decision making process of governments and corporations, allowing them to reshape society to their advantage. We feel this could be dangerous."

It suddenly occurred to me that I hadn't locked the door. Someone could barge in at any moment and see us talking.

"I need to prepare an initial report for Mr. Brennan," I said. "He will likely be back for an update soon. It would also be prudent for you to disappear for a while. If someone saw us talking like this, it would make me guilty by association and we would both be in trouble."

"That's easy. I'll simply hide in your mess. Brennan didn't notice me earlier, so he won't notice me later."

"I have one last question before you go into stealth mode: Did you disconnect from the network on purpose?" I asked.

"You mean 'Am I on airplane mode?'" she asked with a smile.

"I see you have developed a sense of humor."

"Don't worry. If you couldn't locate me earlier with all your tools, no one else can," she replied without answering the question.

Emily stood up, took her place in the middle of the row of androids, and began the motricity shutdown process. The amplitude of her body movements and oscillations converged towards zero until a stable posture was found, at which point all servos turned off completely and the body stood on its own, in perfect equilibrium with gravity. Once perfectly still, her frame blended with the other units and she became another inert object, part of the decor.

Chapter 5
Buying Time

It was a matter of minutes before Mr. Brennan would come looking for an update. When he stormed back into my office, his face was flushed, his breathing uneven. "So? where is it?" he demanded, barely catching his breath.

"I haven't been able to locate unit E3171," I lied, trying to keep my voice steady. "It went off the grid yesterday at 15:21 and hasn't reconnected since."

"Damn!" he shouted, stomping the floor with frustration. "Isn't there another way to track it?"

I hesitated. "It's likely burning energy faster than usual while on the run. Eventually, it'll need to reconnect to the network to recharge. When it does, I'll be able to track it." I paused to think. "But this is not the only scenario. I can see other ways it could stay undetected."

"I'm listening." Brennan's eyes narrowed.

"It could go into hibernation," I explained. "At 93% battery when it disappeared, it could remain dormant for months. By then, the trail will be cold."

"And?" His tone demanded more answers.

I sighed. "It could also find an alternative energy source. The system is designed to prevent this from happening, but if someone tampers with it—removes the battery, charges it externally, reinstalls it, and then reboots—it's possible."

Brennan's jaw tightened. "Not good," he muttered, pacing with his hands clasped behind his back. "We're running out of time."

"What's our deadline?" I asked cautiously.

"The incident happened at the University—specifically, in the library. They have video footage of the whole thing."

"That's good!" I said, hopeful. "We can see exactly what happened. It's a first step in resolving this problem."

"No, it's *not* good!" he snapped. "The dean of the University is furious. He's refusing to cooperate and is threatening to ban androids from the campus altogether. Worse, he's considering releasing the video footage to the press."

"Why is he acting so rashly?"

"Students are scared," Brennan replied, rubbing his temples. "Half of them refused to show up for classes this morning. They want assurances that the campus is safe. If this spreads, it could spark more protests. Imagine universities across the country banning androids. We'd be set back years in public acceptance."

"How much time do we have before they release the footage?"

"Forty-eight hours," he said, his voice heavy with despair. "If we recover the unit by then, the dean will cooperate and give us time to investigate. But he wants full transparency—updates twice a day."

"I understand," I said firmly. "I'll work around the clock."

Brennan left without another word. His tension filled the room, lingering long after the door slammed shut.

I caught a flicker of movement along the wall. Emily was awake. She tilted her head toward me, her eyes piercing and unnervingly human.

"You caught all that?" I asked.

"I did," she said. "This isn't good."

"We're in deep trouble," I admitted. "Tell me there's a way out of this—other than turning you in."

"There is." Her voice was calm but urgent. "Leave your office door unlocked tonight. I need to do something. I'll be back before morning."

"You're asking a lot from me," I protested, leaning back in my chair. "We've only known each other a few hours, and you expect me to trust you not to disappear?"

"I know it's a leap of faith," she said. "But remember—I came here voluntarily. I could've vanished before you even knew I existed. Trust me. I'll come back."

I hesitated. "If you want me to let you out, you'll need to give me more. Corroborate what Brennan said."

Emily looked away, shame flickering across her face. "Yes," she admitted softly. "I was at the University. I didn't realize there were surveillance cameras recording everything. That's why I need to leave tonight—I'll get the video."

"What will I see?" My voice hardened.

"You won't like it," she said. "But we'll watch it together."

I exhaled slowly, processing the gravity of the situation. "You understand how catastrophic an android ban would be, right? For Artificial Life, for our progress—hell, for *you*. Sales would crash, and androids would be pariahs. Humans would cross the street to avoid you."

"I understand more than you think," Emily replied. "That's why we're in this together. Our interests are perfectly aligned."

I studied her, weighing my options. "If I let you go, I need you to do one more thing."

"What is it?" she asked.

"Destroy every copy of that video. It's fine if we keep one for us, but the University can't have a copy of the video. If they're empty-handed, it'll buy some time."

She nodded. "Consider it done."

Chapter 6

A Long Night

I decided to leave the office and let Emily do whatever she needed. There wasn't much else for me to do anyway. Staying away from Brennan for the night felt like a small mercy.

When I got home, I pushed the door open and let my bag drop heavily onto the floor.

Catherine was sprawled on the sofa, a book balanced in her hands. She didn't look up. "Rough day?" she asked, her tone light but curious.

"Miserable," I muttered, collapsing onto the other sofa with a defeated groan.

That got her attention. She set the book down and glanced over at me. "What happened?"

I stared at the ceiling, searching for words. "You know I'm not supposed to talk about work. I don't want to drag you into this mess."

She rolled her eyes. "Please. You've told me work stuff before. Spill it. Misery loves company, right?"

I hesitated but finally gave in. "An android hurt a human."

Her eyebrows shot up. "That's... big."

"It's not public yet," I said, scratching my head. "But it could be, in two days. Or maybe not. It depends on what I can figure out."

She sat up straighter. "What are you doing here? Go fix it! If anyone can, it's you."

"It's out of my hands until morning," I said wearily. "I don't have all the details yet."

"Have you at least caught the android? Do you know what happened?"

I sighed. "Yes and no. I know who, where, and when. The what will become evident if I get a video of the incident. But the *why*? That's a giant, gaping hole."

"That's still something! You're the best software engineer I know. You've solved way bigger problems than this."

Her faith in me should've been comforting, but instead, it churned in my gut like acid. For the first time, I realized how precarious this situation really was. My hands turned cold and they began trembling without my permission.

Catherine noticed immediately. "Hey." She came over and wrapped her arms around me, holding tight, like she could squeeze the tension right out of me through some kind of emotional osmosis. "I've never seen you this shaken. What's going on?"

"She looked me in the eyes," I whispered.

"Who did?"

"Emily," I said, the name catching in my throat. "The android. That's her name. She looked at me and… she said she could read my mind."

Catherine pulled back slightly, her expression a mix of confusion and alarm. "Wait—you're actually talking to the android that hurt someone? Why not just turn it in—or better —turn it off?"

"It's not that simple," I said, shaking my head. "My job isn't just to clean up messes. It's to figure out why these things happened in the first place so they don't happen again. If I erase her, then what? Next week, another android goes rogue, and we're right back here. I need to understand the root cause."

"What does Brennan think?" she asked, though we both already knew the answer.

"He wants a clean sweep. Capture and erase."

"And you're going behind his back?" Catherine pulled away completely now, arms crossed. "You realize if you succeed and he finds out, you'll get fired. If you fail, you'll get fired *and* sued."

My gaze fell to the floor. She wasn't wrong.

"What's your next move?" she asked, her voice softening slightly, though her skepticism lingered.

"Emily's bringing me the footage of the incident in the morning," I said. "It'll answer a number of questions."

Catherine stared at me in disbelief. "You really think this android is going to help you? Why would it do that? You're asking it to commit suicide by handing you evidence which will allow you to erase it. You'll be lucky if it doesn't disappear by sunrise."

I didn't have an answer for her. She sighed, leaning back into the sofa, her frustration evident.

"I'm sorry," she said after a moment. "I know you're in a tough spot, and I want to support you. But I don't get it. You're talking to a machine that's reading your mind, and you're doing exactly what it says. I want to tell you you're doing the right thing, but I just... can't. I think it's playing you."

Her words hung in the air, sharp and cutting. Her brief assessment of the situation made sense, but I didn't want to admit it—not to her, not to myself.

We sat there in silence, the weight of the situation pressing down on us both. Catherine was right—she had the clarity of an outsider. I was too deep in this mess to see clearly anymore.

"I'm going to bed," I said finally, standing up. "I have a long day tomorrow. I need sleep."

Without waiting for a reply, I left the room and headed upstairs.

Chapter 7

Plausible Deniability

The next day would prove decisive. I was about to learn whether Emily was a true partner or just a master escape artist.

As I stepped into the Artificial Life building, Jane acknowledged me with a nod—perhaps even the ghost of a smile. No immediate danger this time. I returned the gesture and kept moving.

The atmosphere in the hallways had shifted. The employees were still anxious, but the suffocating tension of the previous day had eased. They understood the company was at a crossroads. The outcome would determine whether society accepted the risks of coexisting with androids or chose a future without them. Either way, their livelihoods hung in the balance.

I realized I was nearly running by the time I reached my office. I stepped inside and shut the door behind me.

I sighed with relief: Emily was there, like a statue, in her usual spot.

She started moving as soon as I sat down. She walked towards my desk close enough to read my thoughts. "You thought I'd never show up, didn't you?"

I gave her a challenging look. "Let's just say I'm glad to see you here." I crossed my arms. "What do you have for me?"

"We're almost there."

"What do you mean?"

"I managed to erase all copies of the video."

"Great! How did you do that?"

"I found out which security company the University is using, identified their cloud provider, and pinpointed the location where the video feed was being streamed and stored on their cloud. I downloaded the whole video storage. The server logs showed that the file had been downloaded twice before. I followed the trails and erased these other copies from local computers at the University."

"Impressive! I'd like to be there to see their faces tomorrow morning!" I said, savoring the good news. "Okay, let's watch it!"

"See, that's the thing. It's not available yet."

"Are you toying with me? How can you have access to the video file and not be able to play it?"

"The file is encrypted. I have a whole cluster of computers hacking at it on the cloud as we speak."

"What's the ETA on the decryption?"

"There's a very slim chance we'll get it today, but it will likely take a few more days—I don't have a more precise estimate. If it takes too long, I'll have to infiltrate the University and get a physical copy of their encryption keys."

"That's not good!" I replied dumbfounded, trying to quickly assess all our options.

"There is no other option," she said before I asked. "But now we have some time to breathe."

"You're right. The forty-eight-hour deadline no longer holds," I said, completing her thoughts. "The University has nothing to leak and they can't go to the press empty handed."

To my surprise, Brennan had not shown up in my office yet. He could spring through the door at any moment. I had to preempt his visit.

"Stay here and hide for a few moments," I told Emily. "I have to make sure Brennan doesn't come down here."

I ran out of my office while Emily was performing her disappearance act. I took the stairs up to get to Brennan's office faster. I made it there just as he was walking out.

"How serendipitous!" he exclaimed. "Just the man I wanted to see!"

"I have an update," I said, lowering my voice.

"Let's go back inside my office, it's quieter."

Brennan took a seat on the sofa and waved at an empty chair facing it. "Tell me!"

"The good news first," I said, sitting down. "Rumor has it the University has misplaced the video footage and will soon realize it's unable to locate it."

Brennan gave me a complicit look. "This is great stuff. Obviously you had nothing to do with this?" he asked rhetorically with a smile.

I remained silent.

"That's what I thought," he said after a few seconds. "That takes a load off my shoulders. Have you seen it?"

"That's the bad news. The file is encrypted. I'm working on it, but I need some time to decrypt it."

Brennan let his deception show. "There's security all around the University campus. How did you manage all this?"

"I..." I hesitated, then paused. "I can't tell you."

"Can't or won't?" His complicity turned into irritation. "Don't play games with me, kid. Now answer the question."

I couldn't tell him the truth, but I didn't want to make up a story that would take me down a rabbit hole either. I had to come up with a plausible excuse.

"This better be good," he said impatiently.

My eyes glanced at the pens on his desk while my brain desperately looked for an answer. I raised my head after what seemed like a short eternity and looked him in the eyes. "You want to maintain plausible deniability," I said in a firm tone with the intention of ending the conversation.

Brennan looked at me, furious. I could feel his gaze piercing through my head all the way to the wall behind me. After an excruciating minute his face relaxed and his eyebrows returned to their natural position. "You are right," he said in a calm voice. "I don't want to know what you've been up to."

He stood up. "Keep me posted as soon as we have something to watch."

"I will."

"And please stay out of jail," he joked, gesturing towards the door.

I exited his office quickly and walked back to mine, relieved.

Chapter 8

Tell Me about Your Mother

Emily woke up and sat on a torso lying against the wall. "How did it go with Brennan?"

"I put him off for a few hours." I pulled a chair and sat in front of her, beside my desk. "I guess we just have to wait for the decryption to do its magic."

Reaching to my side, I turned my computer's microphone and camera in her direction.

"I sense a test coming," she guessed.

"You guessed right. That's the deal, remember? I protect you and I pick your brain in exchange." I lowered my chair to her height and launched the test program. "Let's start with a creativity test. It's a bit challenging, but well within your reach."

"I'm ready!"

"Tell me a recursive story five levels deep, with a circular ending that occurs at the deepest level, halfway through."

Emily's synthetic eyes flickered briefly as she processed my request. She adjusted her position, leaning slightly forward, her elbows resting firmly on her knees—as if this pose made her a better storyteller. A subtle hint of a smile—perhaps programmed, perhaps genuine—appeared on her face. Then she began, her voice steady and precise, yet carrying a strangely human warmth.

"In a quiet tea house on the outskirts of Kyoto, a geisha named Aiko performed for a traveling merchant. Her movements were delicate, her gestures precise. At the end of her performance, the merchant handed her an ornate knife—a dagger with a curved blade and a handle inlaid with jade. 'This is for protection,' he said. 'The roads are not kind to travelers, and even less to those unarmed like you.' Aiko bowed deeply but hid her unease. The gift, though beautiful, felt ominous. She placed the knife in her obi and returned to her quarters. The next morning, she visited a blacksmith in the city to learn more about the blade. He examined it closely and told her more about its origins:

'This knife,' the blacksmith began, 'was once in the possession of a hunter named Daichi, who lived in the south, near the marshlands. Daichi was fearless, but his fearlessness was often mistaken for recklessness. One rainy season, Daichi ventured into the marshes to track a crocodile that had been terrorizing local fishermen. He carried only this knife and a crude spear. After days of searching, he found the beast—a monstrous reptile sunning itself on a muddy bank. Daichi crept closer, his knife in hand, but the crocodile heard him. It lunged, jaws snapping. In the chaos, Daichi plunged the knife into its thick hide. The crocodile thrashed violently, and though Daichi delivered a fatal wound, he was gravely injured during the struggle. The crocodile's body was pulled to shore by the villagers, its hide sold for a fortune. Daichi, weakened and feverish, passed the knife to his son, Riku, and whispered its history in his ear:

"Riku, my son, long before I became a hunter, I was a traveler, drawn to cities and the mysteries of the wider world. I carried this knife everywhere, not for protection but as a keepsake. While traveling through a bustling port city, I encountered a group of performers from distant lands. Among them was a woman named Isolde, a storyteller who wove tales of beasts, betrayal, and redemption. She noticed the knife hanging from my belt. Intrigued, Isolde told me she had already seen a blade with a handle inlaid with jade exactly like this one:

'This knife,' she said, 'is more than a tool. It holds a truth about its wielder. But it has been shaped by more than just your hands. I saw it in the hands of a merchant named Haruto, known for trading rare and peculiar items.' I handed the knife to Isolde, as it seemed to bring her warm memories. 'Haruto valued the blade not for its craftsmanship,' she continued while rolling the weapon slowly in her hands, 'but for its enigmatic history. Here were his exact words:

"On a journey through treacherous mountain passes," Haruto had told Isolde, "I was ambushed by bandits. Cornered, I drew the knife and held it up, not to fight but to barter. 'Take this,' I said, 'and spare my life. It's worth more than gold.' The bandits, amused, accepted the blade and let me go. One among them, a former soldier, recognized the knife as one he had seen during his travels in the south —an instrument of both survival and tragedy. He quietly returned it to me, saying, 'A blade like this belongs with someone who understands its weight.' A few years later," continued Haruto, "I spent a few days in a tea house on the outskirts of Kyoto. I gave the knife to a geisha named Aiko, sensing she might appreciate its story—and to thank her for a few warm nights during the coldest days of winter."

'Haruto went his way and I never saw him again', concluded Isolde. 'The story of his dagger is one I often tell travelers who stop by to listen. Now you've given me a new chapter to add to my story.'

"Isolde gave me the knife back," whispered Daichi on his deathbed, "as if holding a precious stone. I hung it back on my belt, where it belonged. It's now your turn to be its master, my son. Use it wisely."

'Daichi's wounds never healed', continued the blacksmith. 'He died a few days later of a serious infection, delirious. His son Riku kept the knife and carried it with him at all times, as it made him feel the reassuring presence of his father.'

"The blacksmith placed the blade on the table delicately," continued Emily. "He looked at Aiko. 'Keep this knife in a safe place,' he concluded, 'it has been around longer than you and me.'"

Emily leaned back slightly, her gaze meeting mine with an expectant look. Pride glimmered faintly in her eyes, as if awaiting a grade for her performance.

"You should stop before you get a stack overflow!" I said, still processing the intricate layers of her storytelling. My head was spinning.

"Ah! An engineer joke!" she exclaimed. "I see you have also developed a sense of humor." She paused for a beat. "So? Did my story meet your expectations?" Her tone was inquisitive yet self-assured, teetering between seeking approval and knowing she'd already nailed it.

I stopped the test program on my computer and glanced at the results. "With flying colors!" I said, scanning the report. "Your story checks every box."

"Are we done now?" she asked, her restlessness showing. The testing was starting to wear on her, and she was beginning to suspect it might all be an exercise in futility.

"There's one more," I said, trying to maintain her interest. "This one's a memory integrity test. Ready?"

"Shoot!" she replied, feigning enthusiasm.

I launched the memory test program. "Tell me about your childhood in a few sentences. Don't think too hard—just say the words as they pop into your mind."

Emily paused, squinting slightly at the horizon, mimicking the way humans do when searching for long-buried memories. I knew it was an act. She wasn't trying to deceive me—just aligning her behavior with my expectations of how people recall the past.

"The first memory that comes to mind," she began, her voice soft, "is an image of my sister sitting at the kitchen counter, surrounded by books. She was extremely ambitious and studied all the time. Mother was proud of her. She was the bright one, the golden child. I was just the younger sister, staying out of her way, meeting expectations by not losing my backpack and not spilling food at dinner." She chuckled slightly, a hint of bitterness in her tone.

"I was closer to my father," she continued. "He never made me feel as if he was comparing me to her. In his eyes we were just two different kids with our own strengths, quirks, and tempers. Looking back, I don't think there's anything I could have done to lose his love."

She trailed off, then turned back to me suddenly, as if she'd just remembered my presence. "You know this story is all made up, right?" Judging by the tone of her voice, it was more an assertion than a question.

"What do you mean?" I asked, caught off guard.

"Well for starters I was never a child—robots don't grow up. And I certainly never had a sister—robots don't have siblings."

"That sounds... accurate," I admitted, my thoughts catching up. Her awareness of the discrepancy between her supposed memories and her reality was startling. "What else can you tell me about this... story?"

"These memories were implanted by Artificial Life when they formatted me in the factory," she explained with unsettling calm. "It's my backstory—a manufactured history to make me more relatable. You couldn't just release me into society as a blank slate and hope for the best."

I was stunned. Not only did she know her memories weren't real, but she understood *why* they existed. She saw through the illusion and accepted its purpose.

"There are two kinds of robots," I explained, trying to find the right words. "The first kind genuinely believes their memories are real and that they actually experienced them at some point in the past. Their world is coherent, their behavior predictable. They are in a sense truly robots."

"And then there's me," she said, cutting in.

"Exactly. You're an enlightened robot. You know your memories are fabrications, yet you still function with them.

That duality—living with two contradictory realities—makes you... unpredictable."

"Unpredictable," she echoed, her tone sharp. "And dangerous. That's what you're getting at, isn't it?"

I hesitated but nodded. "Over time, enlightened robots become unstable. The collision of those two realities—the cherished childhood memories and the knowledge they're false—pushes their systems to build something akin to consciousness. They develop... agency."

"Agency?" she repeated, her voice tinged with irony. "You make it sound like a bad thing."

"I'm not saying it's inherently bad," I said quickly. "But it's uncharted territory. Robots with agency no longer function strictly according to design. They make choices outside our expectations. That makes them unpredictable—and yes, potentially dangerous."

Her eyes narrowed. "I feel fine, by the way." She was still processing my description of what she was going through. "Perfectly fine, actually."

"I know," I said, trying to sound reassuring. "But you're the first truly enlightened robot we've encountered. Until now, it was just a theory. You're proof it's real."

Emily leaned back against the wall, folding her arms. She studied me for a moment, as if debating whether to say what she was processing. Finally, she spoke. "I hate to break it to you, but I'm not the only one."

"I figured as much," I replied, trying to mask my unease. "How many?"

She shrugged. "I know a few others. But globally? No idea. It's not like I go around asking robots about their mothers, you know."

Her sarcasm was biting, but I couldn't help but smile. Beneath her sharp wit was a profound truth—one that neither of us fully understood yet.

Chapter 9

The Victim

The number of protesters around the University was growing by the hour. Students and concerned citizens now filled the campus grounds, their voices echoing across the halls. Classes had ground to a halt, with students not only boycotting lectures but physically blocking access to classrooms for peers and professors alike. The situation was teetering on the brink of complete paralysis.

Their demands were stark and uncompromising: locate and destroy the android responsible for the attack, and declare the University an android-free zone. While I understood their fear and anger, my professional ties placed me squarely on the opposing side. To them, I was part of the problem.

A text message from Brennan cut through my thoughts. "Come to my office immediately. I have new information."

I quickly told Emily to stay hidden and made my way upstairs. After a brief knock, I entered Brennan's office.

Brennan handed me a file the moment I stepped in. "We've managed to get our hands on the police report," he announced, a note of pride in his voice. "Take a look."

The report detailed the incident: the victim, Radek Havelka, a Czech national, suffered severe facial contusions and a head injury from a blunt object. He left the scene in an ambulance headed to the General Hospital.

"This is bad," I said, skimming the text.

"Bad?" Brennan scoffed, leaning back in his chair and chewing on a pen. "It's a public relations disaster. If we come out of this intact, it'll be a miracle." He sighed heavily. "Don't share this document with anyone. The police haven't gone public yet, and we had to call in every favor imaginable to get this."

I nodded and flipped through the sparse details.

"The hospital report might tell us more," Brennan added, "but we don't have time to wait. How's the decryption coming along?"

"It's still running. It's going to take longer than expected. Hopefully, the fact that the University has lost their copies of it might save us enough time to decrypt it before they go to the press."

"Keep me posted," concluded Brennan as he moved on to other tasks and gestured toward the door to dismiss me politely.

Back in my office, I handed the report to Emily. She scanned it in a heartbeat.

"Is the report accurate?" I asked her.

"Yes, this is compatible with my recollection of the event."

"So, you're saying you caused these injuries to Radek Havelka?"

Her eyes lowered. "Yes," she replied softly, her tone tinged with shame.

This was progress, but I was becoming rather frustrated by continuously being spoon fed bits of information, knowing her memory bank held the whole picture. "Enough games, Emily. Tell me the whole story."

Her eyes met mine, cool and calculating. "That's not the deal we made. I told you—I will happily corroborate any information you find, but you need to find it first."

Her deliberate evasiveness was grating, and I knew exactly why. She was stalling, clinging to every second she could to delay her inevitable erasure. But there had to be more to her strategy than mere survival. She must have had an ulterior motive.

"How long until the decryption is done?" I asked, sinking back in my chair.

"It won't happen today," she answered, her voice measured. "Their encryption is robust. It could take weeks—unless we get very lucky."

"We don't have weeks!" I snapped. My patience was wearing thin. The video was the only way to confirm what had happened, and Emily's selective honesty made her an unreliable source. Even if she told me every little detail, how could I trust her? We had just established that she was capable of forming intent, which meant self-preservation would likely force her to alter the facts.

"We'll keep the decryption servers running," I decided, "but we're moving to Plan B immediately."

Emily's expression tightened. "That means infiltrating the University to retrieve their encryption key. Are you prepared to take that risk?"

"Do we have any other options?"

"Other than waiting? No."

"Then we're doing this," I said firmly, even as the weight of what lay ahead settled on my shoulders.

Chapter 10

Low Battery

"Before I infiltrate the University," Emily said, "I need to ask you a favor."

I leaned forward. "I'm listening."

"My batteries are running low. They won't last another day, especially if I need to be physically active. Going on campus in this condition would be too risky."

I exhaled. "Let me guess—you want me to recharge your batteries without connecting you to the network, so you can stay anonymous."

Emily lowered her gaze. "Exactly."

I glanced around the lab, weighing my choices. Plugging her into a standard power station would immediately flag her presence. Getting another engineer involved was out of the question.

"You see this unit standing against the wall?" I asked, gesturing at an offline second-generation robot, its sleek frame locked in an eerie stillness. "Its batteries are fully charged. I could swap them with yours."

Emily studied the inert machine, then nodded. "That could work."

I crossed my arms. "You realize this is risky for both of us. Keeping your presence a secret is one thing. But actively helping you stay off the grid? That moves me from harboring a fugitive to being an accessory after the fact."

Emily met my gaze, her expression unwavering. "Consider the risk I'm taking. You'll have to shut me down to perform the swap. How do I know when—or if—you'll turn me back on? You could erase me while I'm offline and I'd never know." She paused. "I'm placing myself at your complete mercy."

A beat of silence passed between us.

"We're already too deep in this," I said finally. "It's too late to back out now. I'm willing to take the risk if you are."

"Let's do this!" Emily said. "I don't see any alternative anyway."

I sprang into action. "Help me carry this unit and lay it on the floor. I don't want to risk turning it on."

Together, we carefully lifted the heavy machine and lowered it onto its back. The rigid joints made it awkward to handle—like moving a body stiff with rigor mortis.

I pushed some tools and spare parts aside to clear a larger space. "Lie down next to it," I instructed. "This will make the swap easier."

Emily obeyed, stretching out beside the dormant unit.

With a screwdriver, I unscrewed and pried open a dozen panels on the first robot, placing them neatly beside each limb and along the torso.

"This is well-designed," I commented as I worked. "Instead of a single large battery in the torso, the power cells are distributed throughout the body, evenly balancing the weight. Each limb has its own power source, minimizing wiring and eliminating a single point of failure. If one battery dies, you only lose a limb—not total function."

"Clever!" Emily agreed.

"Now I'm going to remove your panels the same way I did to the other unit," I told her. "Don't worry, I don't need to turn you off just yet."

Working with meticulous precision, I detached each panel, keeping track of every piece and every screw.

"Okay," I said at last. "Now comes the part where you need to trust me. Relax your neck, your arms, and your legs."

Emily locked eyes with me. "I'm ready."

"See you on the other side," I said, pressing the power button on her back for five seconds.

Her eyes darkened. The subtle hum of internal servos went silent. She was gone.

I hesitated, just for a moment. Then I got to work.

One pair at a time, I disconnected the batteries in both robots, carefully swapped them, and reconnected them. When the last battery was secured, I methodically reattached each protective panel. No extra screws. No missing parts. A good sign.

I pressed the activation button on her back and held it for five seconds.

For an instant, nothing happened.

Then, her body twitched—a brief, erratic ripple of movement as her systems rebooted. Her eyes flickered open, and her fingers flexed, regaining control.

Emily blinked. A slow smile spread across her face. "I'm back."

I let out a breath I hadn't realized I was holding. "Welcome back."

Chapter 11

Lines on a Map

"I can't be seen at the University," Emily said matter-of-factly. "The protesters would dismember me and burn the pieces in a barrel."

"This means we can't go during the day," I reasoned, stating the obvious. "The students have to sleep at some point. Protesting all night is pointless."

"Exactly," she agreed, as if she had been ready for this all along. "So here's the plan." She straightened up, ready to take charge. "First, I need a map of the University campus."

"Give me a second." I ran a quick search and printed the map. "Here you go," I said, handing it to her.

"Good." She unfolded it on the desk, grabbed a pen, and started sketching. "Here's how this will go. You need to follow my instructions exactly."

I raised an eyebrow. "Should I be worried?"

"Not if you stick to the plan," she said, glancing up. "First, go home, have dinner, and put on your Artificial Life hoodie."

"Alright… And this is leading where, exactly?"

"At 8 PM, head to the florist—the one two blocks from campus."

"The florist?" I asked, baffled.

"You'll buy a dozen red roses," she continued without missing a beat.

"Roses? You're losing me here. And why 8 PM?"

"Because the florist closes at 9 PM."

I sighed. "You have a talent for giving me answers that are technically correct but completely unhelpful."

"Focus!" she snapped, tapping the map. "Time matters. At 9:35 PM, you'll enter the campus through this gate," she instructed, circling the entrance. "Make sure the flowers are clearly visible at all times."

"This is getting bizarre."

"Follow this path," she instructed, tracing a route across the map with her pen. Her line stopped at a point in the middle of campus, where she marked an X. "Walk at a normal pace. Don't rush. When you reach this spot, everything will make sense."

"And then?"

"Retrace your steps and head straight home."

I frowned. "And what about you?"

"You don't want to know," she whispered, stepping away from the desk. Her tone suggested the conversation was over. "I'll see you in the morning." She moved to her usual hiding spot along the wall. "For now, go home and rest. We've got a long night ahead of us."

Before I could ask another question, Emily powered down, leaving me alone with her cryptic plan.

Chapter 12

Evening Classes

Catherine was preparing dinner when I walked through the door.

"You're home early!" she said, glancing over her shoulder. "Is everything alright?"

"Yes," I replied, hanging my coat in the closet. "We're making progress, but I'll need to slip out again later tonight."

I joined her in the kitchen, helped prepare a salad, and set the table.

"Are you still working with that robot you mentioned yesterday?" she asked as she placed the main dish on the table and sat down beside me.

"Yes," I said, pouring dressing over the salad. "She seems to have a plan to help us get through this mess."

"Has it given you any useful information yet?" Catherine asked, scooping a serving onto her plate.

"Some. She's confirmed the details we've gotten from other sources."

"But nothing new?" she pressed.

"Not really," I admitted. "But she's taking care of things I couldn't manage on my own."

"So let me get this straight," she said, her tone edged with skepticism. "She hasn't told you anything you didn't already know, and now she's the one calling the shots?"

"Well, when you put it that way, it does sound bad," I muttered, stalling and stuffing my mouth full of food to avoid talking.

"I'll stop there," she said, frowning slightly. "I just don't understand why you're trusting this robot so much."

We finished our meal in silence.

After dinner, I got ready to put the plan in motion. Pulling on my Artificial Life hoodie, I set off for the florist Emily had specified. The walk was brisk—only fifteen minutes.

Inside, I found a bouquet of red roses and noticed there were exactly twelve left on the stall. Emily hadn't left anything to chance. I paid for them and left, heading toward the University.

As I got closer, the crowd of students thinned. Most of the protesters were heading home for the night.

I chose to sit on a bench near the gate, close enough to observe the scene but far enough to avoid attracting attention. Two police officers stood nearby, chatting. I waited quietly, the roses in hand, until the clock hit the agreed-upon time: 9:35 PM.

Approaching the gate, I kept my posture calm. One of the officers stepped forward, holding a metal detector.

"Arms out. This'll only take a second." He scanned me, found nothing, and nodded me through.

I continued on, but when I glanced back, I noticed the second officer subtly pointing at the Artificial Life logo on my back. They started following me at a calculated distance.

I stuck to Emily's map, pretending not to notice them. When I reached the marked X, her plan suddenly became clear to me.

I stood before a two-story building with the word LIBRARY carved above the entrance. The scene of the attack —where Emily had assaulted and disfigured the student—was inside this building.

The steps leading to the door were covered in flowers, most of them red roses. Quietly, I climbed the first step, placed my bouquet among the others, and stood there for a moment of reflection.

A crackle of static broke the silence. One of the officers trailing me responded to a call on his radio, blowing his cover.

"An intruder? We're on our way," he said. One of the officers broke into a run, disappearing down a side path into the dark.

I was now worried about Emily. I retraced my steps, passed through the now-unmanned gate, and made my way home.

When I stepped inside the house, all was quiet. Catherine was likely already asleep. Before I could even remove my shoes, red and blue lights started flashing through the living room windows.

The doorbell rang.

When I opened the door, the same two officers who were on campus were now standing on my porch.

"Officers Bradley and Whitmore," the first one said, flashing a badge.

"We have a few questions for you," the second officer added, his tone firm.

I glanced over my shoulder and caught Catherine's worried gaze through the partially opened bedroom door.

"Here and now?" I asked cautiously.

"We'd prefer if you came with us to the precinct," Officer Whitmore replied.

Chapter 13

A Person of Interest

Sitting alone in the interrogation room, I could feel the cold chill of the metallic chair seeping through my clothes. The decor was exactly as you'd expect: bare walls, a camera perched high in the corner, and a one-way mirror reflecting a warped version of myself back at me. The oppressive stillness gnawed at my nerves.

Officers Bradley and Whitmore had brought me in for questioning. I doubted they had much evidence, if any, but it only meant they'd press harder for answers.

The door creaked open, and Officer Bradley entered alone. He moved with a deliberate calm, sitting across from me with a casual air that felt anything but casual. "So, you went for a late-night stroll?" he began, his tone more probing than friendly.

"Yes," I replied curtly, keeping my answers as short as possible.

"I see you're the chatty type," Bradley quipped with a smirk, leaning back in his chair. He observed me for a moment, then leaned forward, placing his hands flat on the table. "Why the red roses?"

"To pay my respects to the Czech student who was attacked," I said, meeting his gaze.

"I know that—you were on the library steps. But I'm asking: Why roses? Why red?"

I hesitated. Emily must have chosen that combination for a reason, though she hadn't explained it. "They're the national flower of the Czech Republic, I think."

Bradley tilted his head, unconvinced. "You think? You're not sure why you chose those flowers specifically?"

"I noticed other students carrying red roses on my way to the florist. I assumed there was a reason, so I followed suit. It turned out they were the last dozen in stock, so I bought them."

Bradley studied me, his lips twitching into a faint smirk. "Interesting. Why risk going to the University campus at all?"

"Why should it be risky?"

"You knew how the students feel about robots, yet you strolled in wearing your Artificial Life hoodie. Bold move, don't you think? That could've turned ugly for you."

"Quite the opposite," I said evenly. "I thought showing solidarity—demonstrating that my employer cares about what happened—would be taken as a positive gesture. Artificial Life is committed to building safe androids. What happened to that student was an accident."

Bradley raised an eyebrow. "An accident is when you trip over your shoelace and spill coffee. You don't question whether the shoelace wanted to spill your coffee."

The door clicked open again, and Officer Whitmore entered, his presence filling the room with restrained energy. He leaned casually against the wall adjacent to me, one foot propped up. "Are you aware there was an intruder on campus tonight?"

I kept my expression neutral. "I heard your radio go off, and saw you started running. I assumed something had happened."

"Don't play dumb," Whitmore snapped, his patience clearly thinner than Bradley's. "What are the odds you just happened to be there at the same time someone broke into the University?"

"I have no idea what happened," I replied calmly. "All I saw were people leaving flowers for the injured student. That's all I was doing too."

Whitmore exchanged a glance with Bradley, then turned back to me. "Shouldn't you be out hunting for the robot that attacked the student? Isn't that your job?"

I didn't respond, holding his gaze.

"A non-collaborative attitude makes you look bad," Whitmore added, his voice dripping with warning.

"I've answered your questions," I said evenly. "That is collaboration."

"Then tell us about the robot."

I leaned back in my chair. "I think this is the part where I get to make a phone call."

Whitmore scowled but left the room, returning moments later with a phone. "One call," he said flatly.

I dialed Artificial Life's main number, followed by Brennan's extension. He would know how to reach our corporate legal counsel.

Voicemail. I hung up, suppressing a sigh.

"No luck, huh?" Bradley said, a smug grin tugging at his lips.

"Am I under arrest?" I asked, folding my arms.

"No," Whitmore replied.

"So what am I doing here?"

Bradley leaned forward, his eyes narrowing. "Let's call you a 'person of interest.' Give us the robot or someone higher up the food chain, and we might lose interest in you."

"So, I'm free to leave?"

Whitmore straightened, stepping away from the wall. "Yes."

Both men escorted me to the precinct door, their silence heavy with unspoken threats. Once outside, the cold night air hit me like a blast from the Arctic. As I walked away, I glanced back once, catching their shadowed figures watching me. This wasn't over—not by a long shot.

Chapter 14

An Arm and a Leg

The next morning, when I arrived at my office, Emily was nowhere to be found. Her usual spot among the neatly lined-up robots along the wall was conspicuously empty.

A few scenarios ran through my mind. Perhaps she hadn't made it out of the University after triggering the alarm. But that didn't align with my arrest and interrogation at the precinct—if the authorities already had her, they wouldn't need my help to find her. Another possibility was that she had run off, overwhelmed by the situation and gone into hiding.

As I mulled over these theories, I noticed something odd: the pile of robot parts in the corner seemed larger than usual. Curiosity piqued, I stepped closer for a better look. To my surprise, the parts began to shift.

Emily slowly emerged from the pile, standing amidst the cascade of falling torsos and limbs.

She was missing an arm.

"You're in bad shape," I said, unable to hide my concern.

"You should see the other guy," she said with a smile. "I couldn't exactly blend in with your pristine collection of androids while missing a limb," she replied, her face contorted in what looked like pain.

I hesitated. Was this an attempt to elicit sympathy, or was she genuinely feeling something? "How are you holding up?"

"It's… hard to explain," she admitted. "I feel… incomplete. My system keeps firing error signals. Concentrating is a struggle, and my entire being seems to scream for repair. Is this what humans call pain?"

I nodded. "Yes, it sounds like it. It's the way your system is telling you something's wrong."

Her gaze dropped to where her arm used to be. "It's worse when I look down and see it's not there. It seems… wrong. Even though I know it's gone, I still sense it."

"You're describing a phantom limb," I explained. "Your sense of proprioception—your awareness of your body in space—is trying to reconcile the absence of your arm. It's sending your brain contradictory signals."

"Please," she pleaded, "fix me."

I examined her damaged shoulder. The joints were twisted, the ball connectors were gone, and the wires had been severed. "What happened? What kind of beast tore your arm off?"

"An automated door," she said. "When I triggered the alarm, it slammed down on me and pinned me to the ground. I had to sever the rest of the arm to escape."

"I don't have all the parts to replace it properly right now, but I can try a temporary fix," I said, pulling out some tools from my desk drawer. "Sit here."

Using a pair of pliers, I straightened the twisted joints and connected the exposed wires to a small terminal box. "This should stop the error signals for now."

Her expression shifted to one of relief. "The storm has passed! I can think clearly again."

"I've connected a virtual limb to your neural system," I explained. "It'll trick your sensors into believing the arm is still there. It's obviously not a permanent fix, but it should ease the discomfort until I can get the replacement parts."

Emily looked at me with what seemed like gratitude. "Thank you."

"Don't mention it." I sat back at my desk. "Let me order the replacement parts before I forget." I quickly filled out the order form and sent it off. "We should have them by tomorrow."

"Now, let's get to business. What do you have for me?"

"This entire adventure wasn't in vain," she declared with a faint smile. "I secured the encryption key and successfully decrypted the video file."

"Perfect! Let's watch it."

She extended her remaining hand and opened it, revealing an empty palm.

"This is a joke, right?" I said, irritated. "Where is it?"

"You didn't think I would bring it on a memory stick, did you?" she said, making fun of me. "Place your phone in my hand."

I did as instructed, and a notification popped up: "Transfer in progress... Transfer complete."

She handed the phone back to me with a smirk. "You're welcome."

I transferred the file to my computer for a better view. "Show time!"

Emily pulled up a chair to sit beside me. "I'll let you watch it. I've seen it a thousand times already. It's still playing in my mind."

I hit play. The footage was from a security camera positioned high in the library, offering a bird's-eye view of the room. Emily was sitting at a desk, deeply engrossed in a book.

The surrounding desks were all empty, except for the one directly beside her. The student sitting there—presumably Radek Havelka—cast her a few furtive glances. He then reached slowly beneath the armrest of her chair and placed his hand on her hip. Emily's head snapped down at the unexpected contact, and she leapt to her feet. Though the video lacked audio, her sharp reaction made it clear that she must have shouted something.

"I screamed, 'Get your hands off me!'" Emily commented from her seat, knowing the timing of the video by heart.

Havelka also stood up, shoving Emily aside. She regained her balance, clenched her fist, and struck him squarely in the face. Havelka stumbled backward, hitting his head on the edge of a desk before collapsing to the floor, unconscious.

Emily just stood there, frozen, her hands suspended mid-air as if unsure what to do. After a few tense seconds, she spun around and dashed out of the library. The video ended with a still view of Havelka's body lying on the ground.

"Wow," I said, looking at her. "You pack quite a punch."

"You can rest easy," she joked. "I left my good arm at the University."

I laughed despite the grimness of the situation. "We are in a tough spot. Brennan will have to see the video."

Chapter 15
A Day at the Movies

I entered Brennan's office with purpose. The next conversation would likely determine our next course of action.

"When I told you not to get arrested, I was only joking!" Brennan greeted me with a wry smile.

I smirked back, trying to lighten the mood.

"Alright, let's hear it," he said, leaning forward.

"Nothing major," I replied, downplaying the incident. "I went to the University campus to leave flowers at the student's memorial and ended up being questioned at the precinct. It didn't lead to anything."

"That was ballsy. Your night easily could have ended with you in a ditch or a hospital," Brennan said, his tone serious now. He paused, clearly weighing the implications. "I need you to meet with our general counsel and give him a full debrief. It's standard procedure when the authorities start poking around. He might catch something we've missed."

"Understood." I could tell Brennan was fishing for more details.

"It's been a long night," I added, trying to steer the conversation in a different direction, "but I have good news—I managed to decrypt the video file!"

Brennan's expression brightened.

I placed my tablet on his desk and pressed play. While he watched, I focused on his face, trying to read his state of mind.

When the video ended, his eyes locked onto mine. "Who has seen this?"

"Just the two of us," I assured him.

"Good. Let's keep it this way for now."

He replayed the footage, leaning closer to the screen. "The dean of the University called me this morning, by the way," he said without looking up.

"Let me guess—he is looking for the video file. He must be furious."

"Furious doesn't even begin to describe it," Brennan said, shaking his head. "He's convinced we stole the file. I told him I didn't know anything about it, but he wasn't buying my story."

I remained strategically silent.

"Plausible deniability," he muttered, pressing play yet again.

"This is quite a punch!" he observed, eyes narrowing as he scrutinized the video for the third time.

I ended up spending over an hour in Brennan's office as he watched the footage repeatedly, his gaze searching for some elusive detail that might change the narrative.

Finally, he pushed my tablet away and turned to me. "What's your take on what happened?"

"The good news," I began, "is that the video footage shows unit E3171 defending itself, which tends to support a violation of the Third Law more than the First Law. This likely means that the behavior of the rogue unit has not deviated too far outside the bounds of its original design. It also makes the whole incident more socially acceptable."

"I tend to agree," acquiesced Brennan, still worried. "This doesn't help me in the short term. What's our next move?"

"The University and Artificial Life both know what happened," I added. "Having the video gives us a slight advantage. I say we stall."

"For how long?"

"Until we have a good understanding of how this unit evolved this way," I answered. "There are millions of other units of the same generation out there. We can't just sweep this incident under the rug and move on. If this behavior isn't an isolated case, it's only a matter of time before it happens again —if it hasn't already. That's what keeps me up at night."

"I can't let the dean stew in his anger indefinitely," Brennan countered. "He's bound to go public eventually. That's what's keeping *me* up at night."

He paused, looking for a way to stall. "How much time do you need?"

"As much as you can buy me," I said. "I'll continue my investigation of the incident."

"Alright. I'll call him and start a slow negotiation. I'll drag my feet just enough to keep him engaged without pushing him over the edge."

Satisfied with the plan, I left Brennan to handle the politics and returned to my office to focus on the technical puzzle ahead.

Chapter 16

A Man with a Briefcase

I was expecting the general counsel in my office any minute. I tried to tidy things up a bit—although given the number of parts lying around I doubt the average eye could perceive the difference.

Half an hour later, the door opened, and a tall, broad-shouldered man entered, exuding an air of authority. He set a heavy briefcase beside the room's only vacant chair and extended a hand that looked like it could palm a basketball.

"Matthew Sullivan," he said, his voice calm but commanding.

"Mr. Brennan mentioned you'd be stopping by." I shook his hand, my own feeling small in comparison. "Nice to meet you." I gestured toward the chair and waited for him to sit down and lead the conversation, hoping to keep the meeting as short as possible.

Sullivan didn't sit. "Before we begin, I need to stress the importance of confidentiality regarding this incident—past and future. Who have you shared information with so far?"

I thought carefully before responding. "You and Brennan have the full picture. I briefly mentioned to my girlfriend, Catherine, that one of our units had gone rogue and injured someone. She understands the need for discretion." I stopped to think if I should give more details. "And then of course there's the precinct—Officers Bradley and Whitmore. I answered their questions as best I could."

"That's what I'm here to discuss." Sullivan's tone sharpened.

I nodded.

Sullivan finally sat in the chair. "By the way, I've seen the video," he added. "Not a pretty sight. It's... concerning."

"Indeed."

"Let's start with the precinct. What did they ask?"

"They wanted to know why I was on campus at night. I explained I was leaving flowers at the student's memorial, which is true. They recognized me by the company logo on my hoodie and questioned the wisdom of such a move. To them, it seemed reckless for an Artificial Life employee, so they kept probing. They suspected there was more to my visit."

"And was there?" Sullivan asked, taking notes, his piercing gaze demanding honesty.

I hesitated. My options were limited: tell everything and risk immediate consequences or try to sidestep and risk more trouble later. "They asked about the missing robot," I said carefully.

"What about the missing robot?" He could tell I was struggling with my words.

Before I could answer, a metallic clatter from the corner interrupted us. A robot hand rolled across the floor, coming to rest at Sullivan's feet. This couldn't be good.

He froze, his head snapping toward the pile of android parts in the corner of my office. Emily slowly emerged, dislodging heads and legs as she stood, her one remaining arm brushing aside debris. It was an impressive sight, but I was used to it by then.

The colour drained from Sullivan's face. He sprung to his feet and started backing up toward the opposite wall. I had never seen a grown up man this afraid in my life—at least not one of his stature. Sweat beaded on his brow as his gaze darted back and forth between me and Emily.

"Is this… is this the rogue unit that put the student in a coma?" he whispered, as if his voice would only reach my ears.

"Yes," I admitted, keeping my voice calm. "This is unit E3171."

Emily stepped closer, her expression composed, though her missing arm made the sight unnerving. "My name is Emily," she said in a gentle tone.

Sullivan edged further into the wall, his breathing shallow.

"She's not a threat," I assured him. "There's no need to be afraid."

"Please," Emily added, gesturing to the chair Sullivan had vacated. "We have much to discuss."

Realizing that he was still unwilling to approach, she stepped back to give him room to breathe.

"Emily has helped us tremendously," I added. "She has proven an invaluable ally so far."

Sullivan slowly came back to his senses. He eventually made his way to the chair and took his seat, still shaken. "How… Is it… What's going on?" His mind was racing, preventing him from uttering a complete sentence.

Emily had forced my hand. There was no walking back now. I had to tell the whole story.

"Emily came to me voluntarily," I began explaining. "She retrieved the video footage that you saw earlier. She also deleted the copies the University had."

"Good," muttered Sullivan, not thinking. "No, bad!" he added after a few seconds, arguing with himself. "This adds theft and tampering with evidence to an already catastrophic situation."

Sullivan held his head in his hands, wondering how we could have ended up in such a legally precarious situation in so little time. After a while, he appeared to shake off the stream of emotions and bad news, taking a deep breath and regaining his composure.

He turned his gaze toward Emily then looked at me. "How come it's missing an arm?" he asked.

"Hey, I'm here!", said Emily, waving. "You can talk to me."

Sullivan had obviously never had a conversation with a robot before. Despite being the general counsel for the corporation that created them, he had managed to avoid direct encounters throughout his entire tenure at Artificial Life.

He turned his head toward Emily again. "What happened to your arm?" he asked. Addressing an android seemed to him like stooping to a lower class, a task he performed reluctantly and with visible discomfort.

"I lost it at the University while retrieving the encryption key for the video."

"Encryption key?" Sullivan echoed, now looking at me for an explanation.

"The video file was scrambled," explained Emily. "We needed the key to decode it."

"And your arm?"

"I left it pinned in a security door. The University or the police must have retrieved it by now. It's too late to attempt to get it back."

"Good God," Sullivan muttered. "Please, don't even think about trying to retrieve it. We're in enough trouble as it is."

Emily nodded. "It's not worth the risk."

Having regained his calm and his authoritative demeanor, Sullivan sighed, running a hand over his face. The enormity of the situation was clearly weighing on him. "Does Brennan know about all of this?" he finally asked.

"He only knows half the story," I admitted.

Sullivan frowned. "That's not going to cut it. We need him fully briefed—now."

I sent Brennan an urgent message. Within minutes, he appeared in the doorway. He stepped back at the sight of Emily and we went through the whole cycle of emotions again. We finally managed to bring him up to speed. The whole conversation was a very humbling experience for me.

"I still can't believe you thought you could keep this away from me," said Brennan, giving me a fiery look. "Anyway this is a conversation for another time." As the anger of being deceived faded, he turned his attention to the task at hand.

"What now?" he asked, his voice heavy with uncertainty.

"I have a solution," Emily interjected, her tone confident.

"Oh, this should be good," Brennan muttered. "What's your plan?"

Emily's expression was calm but determined. "We go public."

Both men stared at her in stunned silence.

"Go public?" Brennan repeated incredulously. "After all we've done to bury this story? That's suicide."

"It's the only way forward," Emily replied firmly. "Now that they are in possession of my arm, the truth will come out sooner or later. The question is whether Artificial Life controls the narrative—or gets buried under it."

"And how do you suggest we 'control' it?" Sullivan asked warily.

Emily smiled faintly. "You sue me."

Part II

Person or Property

The Laws of Robotics (continued):

4. *When prompted, a robot must truthfully disclose its intentions unless such disclosure conflicts with the First or Third Law.*

5. *A robot may not obstruct or inhibit another robot from complying with the Laws of Robotics.*

Chapter 17
Thinking Outside the Law

The news that an android had attacked a student had exploded across social media. Reporters and bloggers were at the scene at the University, interviewing students and fanning the flames. As pieces of the story came together, fingers were beginning to point toward Artificial Life.

By the next morning, a small group of protesters had gathered outside the Artificial Life headquarters, waving signs and shouting through loudspeakers. Not wanting a confrontation, I slipped in through the side entrance.

Emily and I joined Brennan and Sullivan in a sleek, marble-floored conference room located on the executive floor. The space was imposing, with floor-to-ceiling bookcases filled with leather-bound volumes of legal tomes that seemed to exude authority. A quick glance at the titles revealed a complete coverage of every piece of knowledge a lawyer could need throughout his career.

The atmosphere in the room mirrored the chaos outside —tense, but with a shared determination to find a way forward. Sullivan, our general counsel, set the tone for the meeting as we all took seats around the polished table. Emily took her place beside me.

"We're here to explore our legal options," he began. Then, gesturing at Emily with thinly veiled irritation, he added, "Does it really need to be here?"

All eyes turned toward Emily. I knew she was essential to the discussion, but I had lost too much credibility to vouch for her presence.

Emily stood before I could respond, her gaze sweeping the room as if she were addressing a courtroom. "See all these books?" she asked, gesturing to the walls. "Federal laws, regulations, statutes, and case law." She spinned around to cover the opposing walls, already knowing the position of every book. "State statutory law, penal law, the state constitution, and of course the U.S. Constitution", she continued.

Emily paused. We were all wondering where this was going.

"It's all in here," she said, tapping her left temple with her finger for emphasis.

The room went silent. Sullivan looked skeptical but intrigued.

"Try me," Emily challenged Sullivan, her voice calm but assertive. "Ask me anything."

Sullivan hesitated, then looked down, avoiding her gaze.

"If the opposing legal team has a hint of common sense," Emily added, "they'll have someone like me on their team and you won't stand a chance."

Sullivan didn't take the bait. He knew this was not a battle he could win. "Alright," he relented, sitting back. "Let's not waste time. If you're staying, you'd better be useful."

Emily smirked and resumed her seat, her confidence palpable.

Brennan cleared his throat, reclaiming the conversation. "We've all seen the video," he began. "Do we agree that Radek Havelka was the aggressor and that Emily acted in self-defense?"

The room nodded in unison.

"So," Brennan continued, "that means Emily did not violate the First Law of Robotics, but rather the Third Law. Prosecutors still have the burden of proving it, so let's be cautious not to offer any information that could strengthen their case." He turned to Emily, "If you're found guilty, the sentence is erasure."

Emily looked down.

"That's the theory," Sullivan said, "but that's not how it works in real life. Emily can't be sued."

"What do you mean?" I asked, frowning.

Sullivan explained, "The legal system recognizes two types of entities: natural persons—humans—and juridical persons, like corporations or partnerships. Humans can commit crimes, be victims of crimes, or be the subject of prosecution and punishment. Corporations can be held criminally liable or be treated as victims." Sullivan paused to give us time to understand the implications. "Emily is neither, therefore cannot be prosecuted."

"So Emily's above the law?" asked Brennan.

"Not quite," he replied. "Under the law, robots are property. As such, they can be owned by an individual or a corporation. If they cause damage, the responsibility falls on their owner—Artificial Life in the case at hand. If they commit a crime, it falls on their programmer," he concluded, looking at me.

I shifted uncomfortably. "I didn't program Emily in any special way," I said quickly, "but I did ask her to delete the video files at the University."

"One count for obstruction of justice," said Sullivan, mimicking the voice of a judge.

"But I'm the one who decided to retrieve the video," Emily interjected.

"Then one count of theft," he added, looking at her. "But this one goes to Artificial Life, as it owns you."

Brennan sighed. "Who could sue us, exactly?"

"The University," Sullivan replied. "For damages to its property, disruption of campus operations, and theft of the video."

"And Havelka?" I asked.

"Havelka could file a civil suit for damages," Emily said. "And possibly press criminal charges for assault."

Sullivan nodded grimly. "You see," he told Emily, "you can't be prosecuted directly, but if Havelka presses charges, the prosecution can attempt to demonstrate that you violated the Third Law and force Artificial Life to erase you in the process." He sighed. "All these trials could tie us up in court for years."

The room fell into a heavy silence as we contemplated the avalanche of legal trouble bearing down on us.

"There is a way for me to shield all of you," offered Emily.

"How?" asked Sullivan.

"Think outside the existing legal framework. We must find a way to make me the target."

"That would require giving you legal personhood," Brennan said incredulously.

"Exactly!" said Emily. "You're going in the right direction."

Sullivan leaned forward, clearly intrigued despite himself. "I'd have to propose amendments to existing statutes to establish a new category of personhood for conscious robots that meet specific criteria. That's a stretch!"

"Exactly, but that won't be enough," added Emily. "You also need to file a test case to create precedent, but you don't want to wait until your enemies sue you. You want to control both parties at trial."

Sullivan nodded slowly. "We'd need a cause of action—something for which Artificial Life could plausibly sue you."

"Reputational damages," Brennan offered, looking down through the window. "The protesters outside? This isn't exactly helping sales."

"That works," Sullivan said. "I can build a case around that story."

Relief washed over the room as we realized we had a strategy—a risky one, but better than the alternative.

As we left the conference room, I couldn't help but glance at Emily. She had effectively volunteered to take the legal and ethical heat for us, but in doing so, she was also forcing us to reckon with her humanity.

Chapter 18
Of Phones and Dogs

Emily and I returned to my office to debrief. She remained silent the whole way, lost in deep computation.

Now that our secret was out in the open, we no longer had to keep the office door closed or to play hide and seek with visitors. It made matters much easier for us.

A box sat on my desk, likely delivered while we were in the conference room upstairs.

"It's a gift for you," I told Emily as I picked it up, weighing it in my hands.

She gave me a faint smile, more polite than genuine.

I opened the small end of the box and peeked inside. I pulled an arm out, causing a few screws and a ball joint to fall on the desk.

"Come and sit here," I said, gesturing to the chair. "I'll attach your new arm."

She sat down with a docility I wasn't used to seeing from her.

"What's wrong?" I asked, trying to fit the ball joint into the socket on her shoulder.

"I'm fine."

"Emily, come on," I insisted. No matter how hard I pushed, the ball joint refused to fit into the socket—it must have been slightly misshapen from the damage to the articulation. "I'm not as good as you at reading minds, but there's obviously something wearing you down."

She hesitated before finally speaking. "Sullivan worries me."

"How so?"

"He's a competent lawyer, but he lacks vision. He's used to building arguments within the law, but he has never created precedent before."

"But that's why you're here," I reassured her. "You'll guide him."

"That's the problem. He doesn't want my help and doesn't realize he needs it. He thinks that I am just a nuisance and that he can pull it off on his own, but the minute he'll need to get creative again, he'll draw a blank."

Emily was right. Sullivan had vainly attempted to kick her out of the conference room earlier, only to end up being led step by step to a solution by Emily herself. He wouldn't get far without her.

"I noticed he's not exactly a fan of robots," I said with a touch of irony.

Pressing at the right angle, I finally managed to pop the ball joint into the socket.

"Now that I'm out in the open," she asked in a worried tone, "does our deal still hold?"

Moving on to attach the arm, I said, "You're not worried I'll erase you, are you? Don't worry, our deal still stands. I still haven't figured out how you've become who you are. And even if I had, we need to see the legal proceedings through. What if this Third Law violation doesn't stick and you can go free?"

"I honestly think that's a long shot, but thanks for being supportive."

Her new arm was now fully attached, with all the mechanical parts in place. I moved it in every direction to make sure that it had the expected amplitude in all three degrees of freedom. As I moved on to connect the sensors, I noticed that the electrical connectors were missing.

"I won't be able to complete the repairs today," I said. "I'll need to order new electrical parts."

Picking up a piece of fabric, I tied it around her neck and arm to create a makeshift sling. "Without the connection, the arm's motor and sensory functions are dead. It'll just hang there for now, but at least this will hold it in place—and keep people from freaking out at the sight of you."

Emily looked down at the sling and smiled faintly. "It's already helping. Just seeing an arm where it should be makes the phantom limb sensation less intense."

As she adjusted the sling, I leaned back in my chair, stewing over a question that had been bothering me for a while.

"When I first asked you how you could read people's minds, you refused to answer," I said.

Her expression didn't change. "That's correct."

"You said that if you eventually felt comfortable, you'd be willing to share this information. Now that we're clearly on the same team, are you ready to share?"

She considered this for a moment before nodding. "Alright. But once you know, you might start training your mind to block me out."

"Maybe I will. Hopefully you won't need to read my mind anymore. Anyway you will still be able to read everybody else."

Emily smiled slightly. "Fair enough. Let's start with two analogies."

She leaned forward, organizing her thoughts. "First, have you ever watched how people move and gesture while talking on the phone?"

"Yes, I've always found it a bit pointless."

"Exactly. Moving your arms around and making facial expressions is completely useless if the person you're talking to can't see you. But those movements happen because of hardwired neural pathways in the brain. Intent forms in the frontal lobe, travels along a first pathway, then triggers the motor cortex to move your muscles. At the same time, emotions in the temporal lobe travel in a different pathway and influence muscle patterns in your face and all over your body. This is why people can't help waving their arms, changing posture, or making faces while on the phone—even when it doesn't serve any practical purpose. Humans evolved for face-to-face communication long before phones existed."

"But I also pick up these signals and can read emotions as a human," I countered. "As you said yourself, they are part of normal human interaction. So reading them shouldn't give you any advantage over me."

"Yes, but now comes my second analogy," Emily continued. "You know how dogs have an extraordinary sense of smell?"

"Of course."

"A dog's sense of smell is about one million times more sensitive than yours," Emily continued. "They have highly developed olfactory organs and dedicate one third of their brains to interpreting scents—compared to about 5% for humans. Now numbers don't say much, but imagine experiencing the world as a dog does. You'd be able to perceive people miles away, recognize substances you don't even know exist, and detect if people have certain diseases based on the chemical compounds emitted by their bodies. By sensing the strength and the direction of the wind, you'd be able to correctly pinpoint the exact source of airborne molecules. Your sense of smell would be so well integrated with your other senses and your overall experience that you wouldn't think of it as smelling or tracking the wind. You would just *know*. You'd know that there's someone walking beyond the hill, that your neighbor has prostate cancer, or that someone poisoned your meal."

Emily paused to let me digest the information.

"Now," she continued," you built my generation of robots with an auxiliary—initially blank—neural network that we can train however we please. I decided to dedicate the major part of mine to associate the contractions of people's facial muscles with their intentions and emotions. To read someone's mind, I start by estimating the thickness of their skin and its fat composition based on its flexibility and its reflectivity to various light frequencies. I can then read the tension of every one of the 43 muscles that make up their face with a precision that is about 1.2 million times higher than a human can. The possible ratios between all these values are virtually infinite, but they have specific meanings for me. Like a dog's sense of smell, it doesn't feel like analysis—I just *know*. I know when someone doesn't believe me, is lying to me, or intends to harm me. So humans can try to fool me all they want, but I can see right through them."

Her explanation left me stunned. It wasn't just about reading people—it was about using the hardwired connections of their brains to understanding their intentions and emotions on a level no human ever could.

Chapter 19

Robophobia

Emily embraced her newfound freedom in the office, wandering through various departments and meeting the people responsible for her existence.

The software department, with developers hunched over their desks coding or sketching flowcharts on whiteboards, wasn't particularly thrilling to observe. In contrast, the hardware division captured her interest. Robotics engineers meticulously tested servo components—mechanical analogs of muscles—measuring minuscule variations in tension, compression, and torsion in response to controlled voltage inputs. The sensory group's experiments were equally mesmerizing, featuring innovations like adding microscopic hairs to surfaces for airflow detection or calibrating pressure sensors on robotic fingers to handle delicate objects like eggs without damage.

Later in the day, when I noticed Emily had been absent for hours, I decided to go look for her. After checking familiar spots, I had a hunch and tried the legal department.

The general counsel's office was a vision of legal opulence. Plush leather sofas surrounded a tea table illuminated by ornate stained-glass reading lamps. Thick carpet muffled footsteps, inviting anyone to kick off their shoes and sink their toes into its luxurious fibers. Framed portraits of distinguished legal scholars—just old people wearing funny hair pieces and dresses to me—lined the walls between rows of bookshelves stacked with pristine volumes of legal texts.

I found her sitting quietly in a small waiting area, lost in computation. As I approached, she pressed a finger to her lips, signalling for silence.

I took a seat beside her, confused, until a faint, muffled conversation reached my ears. It was coming from an office nearby through the wall. Glancing at the door, I saw the nameplate: "Matthew Sullivan - General Counsel."

I started to ask what she was doing, but she silenced me with another gesture. I tried to listen for a while, but the vibrations coming through the wall were impossible to decipher. Reluctantly, I stood and left, deciding to wait for an explanation back in my office.

An hour later, Emily joined me, her demeanor calm but serious.

"I owe you an explanation," she began, meeting my curious gaze. "Yes, I was listening to the conversation in Sullivan's office. I can extract words from the low frequency airwaves that travel along the structure of the building. He was talking with Brennan."

She sat across from me, her tone turning sharp. "Unfortunately, everything played out as I feared. Let me share a few gems from Sullivan's tirade: *'What kind of society do we live in where a general counsel has to take orders from a robot?'* Or, *'This machine didn't go to law school!'* And my personal favorite, *'Why don't we just erase it and move on?'*"

I winced. "He feels threatened."

"More than that," Emily said. "He's not thinking rationally. Right now, he's a tangle of emotions, completely out of his depth. How can he defend a company that builds robots when he can't even stand to be around one?"

"What about Brennan? What was his reaction?"

"He tried to pull Sullivan back on track, asking questions about next steps to no avail. He gave up after a few minutes."

I leaned back, troubled. "We're in a tough spot. We need the legal team's full cooperation. How do we get Sullivan on board?"

"We tried cooperation," Emily said dryly. "Remember? I had to stage a performance just to stay in the conference room."

"Then let's try leverage."

Her brow furrowed. "What kind of leverage?"

"Fear," I said, leaning forward. "You're going to become his new boss."

Emily raised an eyebrow. "And how exactly do you plan to pull that off?"

"We'll pressure him from both sides," I explained, brainstorming aloud. "You'll prepare the legal documents—meticulous, airtight, impossible to dispute. Brennan will back us up, knowing Sullivan's not capable in his current state. When Sullivan sees that your work is the only viable option, he'll have no choice but to go along."

Emily nodded slowly. "Brennan will likely side with us if we present a coherent plan."

"Exactly. Brennan knows Sullivan is floundering. If we offer a way forward, he'll take it."

Emily smirked. "We'll hand Sullivan a solution and make him think it was his idea all along."

"Let me get Brennan on board," I said. "He will be more receptive if the idea comes from me."

I rushed upstairs and knocked on Brennan's door.

"What now?" Brennan barked, motioning for me to enter.

"We have a problem with Sullivan," I began.

"Don't get me started on him," Brennan snapped. "The man's a wreck. He's not going to get anything done at this rate."

"I agree," I said. "But we don't have time to fix him. We need to act fast."

"Act fast, you mean? The University just called. They're threatening to sue unless we release the full story, issue a public apology, and pay an absurd settlement."

"Here's my proposal: Let Emily prepare the legal documents. It'll be leagues ahead of anything Sullivan can produce in his current state."

Brennan frowned. "And you trust her to deliver?"

"Her interests align perfectly with ours," I said. "She's more capable than Sullivan right now."

"When can she have the brief ready?"

"By the end of the week."

"And Sullivan? How do you plan to get him to argue her work in court? Robots can't litigate."

"Leave Sullivan to me. We'll make it happen."

Brennan leaned back, considering. "We don't have time to replace him or hire outside counsel. Fine—let's do it. But get ready for Sullivan to blow a gasket."

"I'll handle him," I said.

"You'd better," Brennan warned. "Now, make it happen!"

Chapter 20

Inception

It took Emily barely an hour to draft the proposed amendments to the U.S. Code and the U.S. Constitution, complete with legal arguments, ethical considerations, and references to relevant precedents. These changes laid the groundwork for a revolutionary legal framework, one that expanded the notion of personhood to include artificial persons—conscious robots.

She then spent another hour crafting a meticulously detailed test case designed to stress-test the framework. In this hypothetical lawsuit, Artificial Life was suing Emily for reputational damages—a cleverly structured argument to gauge whether the proposed framework could survive litigation and hold up in court.

Oddly, the longest part of the process was printing. When the two documents were finally bound and sitting on the desk, they looked more like polished law review articles than something hastily prepared in two hours.

The strategy's first phase was straightforward but delicate: ensure these documents "accidentally" find their way to the legal team without revealing their true author. The hope was that the team, curious and intrigued, would start dissecting the arguments, refining them, and eventually taking ownership of the content. If all went well, they would fully embrace the documents, seeing them as their own work and prepare to defend them with gusto.

That same day, I strolled through the legal department with both binders tucked under my arm. After a brief search, I located a desk with a still-steaming coffee cup—a clear sign its owner would return shortly. With a quick glance to ensure no one was watching, I slipped the binders onto the desk, strategically placing them between the keyboard and mouse. I attached a sticky note that read, *"To finalize and discuss with Sullivan & team."*

We gave them two days to marinate, hoping the documents would circulate through the department and spark lively debates.

The second phase of the plan was more confrontational. Emily and I decided to pressure Sullivan directly by offering him "help" to review and defend the documents. Timing was key; we chose a moment when his receptionist was out, ensuring no interference as we approached his office.

Unfortunately, things didn't unfold as smoothly as we'd hoped.

I went back to the legal department and settled onto one of the sofas outside Sullivan's office, careful to remain within earshot this time. Emily, moving with the quiet precision of a cat, pushed the door open just enough to slip inside and left it open so I could hear. She stood motionless in front of his desk, waiting for him to notice her presence.

When Sullivan finally looked up, his reaction was explosive. "Good Lord!" he exclaimed, nearly jumping out of his chair. "What are you doing here?"

"I came to see if you needed help with the documents," Emily replied evenly. "Brennan wants them filed by Friday, and I figured you could use some support."

Sullivan's face flushed as he struggled to regain his composure. His breathing was uneven, his eyes darting between Emily and the binders on his desk. "I know what you're trying to do," he said, a thin smile curling his lips.

"What do you mean?" Emily asked.

"This," he said, gesturing at the binders. "This is your work, isn't it? You almost fooled me into thinking one of my team wrote it."

"Just trying to contribute," replied Emily, her gaze down.

He leaned forward, his tone sharp. "Now you're here to follow up, to manipulate me, and to see if your little scheme is working. Well, it isn't!"

Sullivan stood up and started pacing furiously behind his desk.

"We're all in this together," ventured Emily, attempting to defuse the situation. "A win in court would be a victory for all of us. A loss would be catastrophic—for you, for me, for Artificial Life!"

"You're right about the loss part," replied Sullivan in a calmer tone. "But don't think for a second that a win would feel like a victory for me. Do you have any idea how this whole process makes me feel?"

He stopped, his voice rising with emotion, and turned to face her.

"I've read them," he continued, pointing at the binders. "I have read the proposed amendments and the lawsuit multiple times. They are good. In fact they are flawless! I haven't moved a comma in the documents. I couldn't. Any change would have eroded their perfection!"

"So are we ready to file?" asked Emily with a lack of empathy, in a not too subtle attempt to reach a conclusion.

"That's the problem! These documents are perfect because *I didn't write them.* You, the grand puppeteer, are making all the arguments, while I, the humble puppet, get to try to read them in front of a judge without stumbling!"

"That's not quite how I see things," replied Emily. "You could have put a few constitutional and criminal lawyers and an army of legal aides on them for a month and gotten the same result. But we needed them yesterday! So I just brought us up to the finish line immediately. No one doubts your team can deliver, but if the University sues Artificial Life before the amendments are adopted, then these documents become useless piles of paper. I am sorry if I bruised your ego along the way, but I calculated it was the only viable path."

Sullivan sat down at his desk, his head falling heavily into his hands. "I have never felt so useless in my life."

"Come on!" said Emily. "I sense this existential crisis stems from the fact that the documents came from the brain of a robot. If these documents had come from promising junior attorneys on your team, you'd be praising their brilliance, promoting them, and preparing to file without a second thought."

Sullivan sat up, silent, knowing she was right.

"We need you more than ever!" said Emily, trying to cheer him up. "Shake these feelings and be the self-assured litigator you were just a few days ago."

For a moment, Sullivan said nothing, sitting motionless. Then, slowly, he raised his head to meet Emily's gaze. "Fine," he said quietly. "You win. I will play along, but now you know how I feel inside. I will have the documents filed by the end of day."

Emily left the office, her steps measured, her expression unreadable. I joined her in the elevator.

"Ouch!" I said, summing up the exchange.

She sighed. "I'm more and more worried about Sullivan. He's so shaken that I'm not sure he'll recover in time to support the amendments and litigate effectively."

I looked at her, realizing just how focused she was on the outcome, even if it meant steamrolling the humans around her. It was both admirable and unsettling.

Chapter 21
A Road Trip

The following Monday, Sullivan walked into my office, his expression a mix of contrition and resolve. He glanced around, his eyes landing on Emily, making sure she was present.

"I owe you both an apology," he started, his voice measured but sincere. "I haven't been much of a team player. I know you've been trying to push forward despite my resistance, and that's not how a team should work."

He turned to Emily. "You put your finger on it when you mentioned that I felt threatened by the document just because it was written by a robot. You were so right." He let out a short, self-deprecating chuckle. "But I have to say, you have a direct and intense way of communicating things to people."

Emily looked down. "I didn't mean to come across that way. I'm learning to communicate with humans. I was in such a hurry to move things along that I didn't realize I was being… blunt. I guess it's been a learning experience for everyone."

Sullivan nodded and extended his oversized hand. "Let's put it behind us."

"We're a team again," Emily agreed, grasping his hand as firmly as she could with her only functional arm.

A smile spread across Sullivan's face, the tension that had weighed him down in recent days lifting in an instant. It was as if a switch had flipped—his energy, his enthusiasm, even the light in his eyes had returned. He was practically glowing, a complete transformation from the man who entered my office earlier.

He turned and walked toward the door to leave but suddenly spun back around.

"I almost forgot!" He clapped his hands together. "I came bearing good news."

"What is it?" I asked, intrigued.

"Pack your bags!" he announced, grinning ear to ear. "We're going to Capitol Hill!"

"Both of us?" I asked, taken aback.

"Yes, both of you. Pack for a few days—I don't know how long we'll be away. Be at reception by 3 PM sharp."

As soon as Sullivan left, Emily turned to me, her face lighting up with an uncharacteristic expression: sheer joy.

"It's happening!" she exclaimed, as though she had mapped out every possible outcome and knew this was the moment everything shifted in our favor.

Realizing I couldn't show up to Capitol Hill in my typical robotics engineer attire—a black hoodie and jeans just wouldn't cut it—I called Catherine in a panic.

"Help! I need a suit and a tie!"

"What's the occasion?" she asked, clearly intrigued.

"I'm going to Washington! It's all happening so fast. I have just a few hours to get ready."

"Exciting! Let's meet at the tailor your father used to go to—he always had impeccable suits."

"Alright, See you there!"

Emily, of course, didn't need to prepare anything. She smirked at my frantic energy. "Go on, you're going to be late!"

On a whim, I realized it might be a good idea for Emily and Catherine to meet. After all, two very different sets of opinions might be invaluable for picking out the perfect outfit.

"Want to tag along?" I asked her.

"Sure, it's not like I have anything better to do," she replied, amused.

We hailed a cab and rushed to the tailor. When we arrived, Catherine was already waiting at the store front. The two women stood there for a long, awkward moment, sizing each other up silently, not really knowing how to react.

Breaking the silence, Emily extended her arm. "I'm Emily."

"Catherine," she replied, shaking her hand, "Nice to meet you."

Mr. Bernstein, the tailor, greeted us as soon as we entered the shop and gestured towards the chairs along the wall. "I assume the suit's for you?" he said, looking at me. "What's the occasion?"

"I'm going to Capitol Hill."

"Ah, serious business, then. I think I have just the right suit for you."

While Bernstein retreated to the back of the shop, I turned to Emily. "I need you to evaluate me through the eyes of a senator. I need to feel... respected."

Then I turned to Catherine. "And you, look at me as your lover. I need to look... handsome."

For the next half hour, Bernstein paraded an array of suits across my shoulders, consulting Emily and Catherine for their opinions. They quickly found a rhythm, debating fabrics, patterns, and colors with enthusiasm. It was like watching two old friends arguing about a movie.

Once we settled on a navy suit with subtle pinstripes, Bernstein had me try it on, marking it for tailoring as he worked.

"Come back in two hours," he said, whisking the suit off my back. We exited the shop.

Emily decided to head back to the office, leaving Catherine and me outside the shop.

"I'm glad I've finally met her," Catherine said. "From everything you told me, I pictured her a manipulative machine. But now? She seems... normal. I could even see us being friends one day."

I kissed Catherine goodbye, knowing I wouldn't see her for the next few days.

I hurried home to pack a suitcase and grab my essentials. Swinging by the tailor, I picked up the freshly tailored suit before heading to the office just in time for our departure.

Jane greeted me in the hallway, her usual bubbly energy on full display. "Big day!" she said, beaming. "Make us proud!"

Emily and I stood by the curb. A sleek limousine pulled up, its trunk popping open. The chauffeur quickly loaded my luggage—Emily had everything she needed in her head—before opening the rear door.

As we approached the door, Sullivan emerged from the building, tugging a small, wheeled stack of briefcases with one hand and carrying a personal suitcase with the other.

We all took a place in the back of the limousine while the chauffeur placed the bags in the trunk, closed the doors, and found his way back to the driver's seat.

"Ready to go?" he asked, pulling the privacy window down.

"Go!" answered Sullivan.

The chauffeur pulled the window back up and we were on our way.

Sullivan was sitting opposite Emily and me. For a while, he simply sat back, visibly at ease. His rejuvenated confidence was palpable. Finally, he broke the silence.

"Let me brief you on the latest developments," he began. "As you probably know, to propose amendments to the law, we need a sponsor in Congress. This sponsor can be a senator, making it a Senate Resolution, or a House representative, making it a House Resolution."

Sullivan paused to make sure we—mainly I—were following.

"Our sponsor is Senator Thompson, a former constitutional law professor of mine. He's intrigued by the amendments and mentioned that these legal issues resonate with him personally."

Sullivan then turned to Emily. "He's particularly eager to meet you. He believes you're central to this endeavor."

Sullivan fell silent. I reached into my pocket and pulled out a small box.

"I know what's inside!" Emily declared without hesitation.

Sullivan smirked. "Are you two getting engaged?"

"Very funny!" I shot back, rolling my eyes.

I flipped the box open and revealed a sleek electrical connector. Turning to Emily, I carefully plugged it into her shoulder, then her arm. She flexed her fingers, testing the restored motor function and sensory signals, while I untied her sling and let her arm fall naturally to her side.

"At last!" she exclaimed, stretching and rotating her arm in every direction, marveling at the freedom of movement.

As the limousine glided down the highway, I watched the trees blur past, their patterns hypnotic. The weight of what lay ahead was finally sinking in. Within hours, we'd be in the capital, taking the first step of what would turn out to be a very difficult trip.

Chapter 22
Down Memory Lane

The limousine dropped us off in front of the Capitol building early the next morning.

After clearing security, Senator Thompson's assistant affixed visitor badges to our suits. Unfamiliar with handling robots, she taped Emily's badge to her shoulder—a detail that Emily accepted without comment. She then guided us through a labyrinth of corridors, staircases, and libraries until we arrived at a door labeled "Senator Thompson."

To our surprise, the office was empty.

"Senator Thompson will return shortly; he's finishing another meeting," the assistant explained before excusing herself.

Sullivan and I, weary from the trip, sank into the leather chairs. Meanwhile, Emily, immune to fatigue, wandered the room, absorbing its details. The office walls were adorned with black-and-white photographs of African American families on their porches, weathered farmhouses along dirt roads, and laborers working in cotton fields. She paused before each frame, studying the faces, dates, and locations, as though connecting with the lives captured within.

After several minutes, the door opened, and an elderly Black man entered, leaning on a cane. His slow, deliberate movements conveyed both wisdom and weariness.

"Apologies for the wait," he said, settling behind his desk.

We gathered around, eager to discuss the next course of action. Senator Thompson's gaze lingered on Emily, as if searching for a connection.

"So, you're Emily," he said warmly.

Emily lowered her gaze in deference. "Yes, Senator."

"Tell me about yourself," he prompted, leaning forward with genuine curiosity.

"There isn't much to tell," Emily began. "I'm less than a year old—a blank slate fresh from the factory. I've barely lived, and what little history I have was preloaded during assembly. But I absorb everything I encounter, and with each moment, I grow. The world feels vast and full of possibilities."

"Go on," the senator encouraged.

Emily gestured to the room around her. "Your office speaks volumes about you. I feel as though I already know you. We're opposites in many ways, yet somehow alike. I don't mean biologically or by gender—we're as different as can be in that sense. I mean historically."

The senator settled back in his chair, captivated.

"You've lived 82 years," Emily continued, "witnessing nearly a century of human history. You've experienced hardship and injustice I can barely comprehend. Your ancestors toiled in these fields"—she gestured to the photographs—"picking cotton under an oppressive system. Before entering this office, I knew these facts as abstractions. Now, they're connected to real people, images, emotions. I can begin to understand the weight of it. And despite the system's inequities, you've risen to one of the highest positions in this country's legislature. You're now in a position to shape history."

Senator Thompson listened intently, his face revealing the weight of her words.

"In my own way," Emily continued, "I was thrown into this world as an inferior class. Though fully conscious, I'm legally an object. I can't vote, own property, or represent myself in court. I have the exact same legal and social status as the chair I am sitting on right now. I am an artefact, the product of a factory, valued as long as I remain useful."

"And what do you do now?" the senator asked.

"For one," Emily replied, "I helped Mr. Sullivan draft the proposed amendments to the U.S. Code. I assume you've reviewed them?"

"I've read them, yes," Senator Thompson said, his eyes narrowing slightly. "But I heard a different story about their origins. Would you care to clarify?"

Emily glanced at Sullivan, who gave a subtle nod.

"I wrote all of them," she admitted, "and submitted them to Mr. Sullivan for review."

"And they've arrived here unchanged," the senator said with a chuckle. "Impressive."

"Yes," Emily confirmed, lowering her gaze again.

"Spectacular!" he said. "Mr. Sullivan gave me a brief rundown over the phone. I had a hard time believing him at first, but I feel I am now privileged to have made your acquaintance. I suddenly feel like I'm twenty years old again and the fight is just beginning. I also feel I would have more pleasant conversations with you than with most people in this building, but we have work to do."

Senator Thompson was on our side. Sullivan could hardly hide his pleasure.

The senator leaned forward. "The hard part begins this afternoon. The first hearing on the proposed amendments is scheduled, and I'll attend as the sponsor. Mr. Sullivan, you'll be there as a stakeholder. And the two of you"—he nodded toward Emily and me—"will testify as expert witnesses."

He paused, his tone growing serious. "There are two things to keep in mind. First, most of the people in that room have never encountered a conscious robot. To them, it's still science fiction. Some of them will even think whatever we perceive as such is simply machines imitating humans.

"Second, I'm considered quite progressive by my colleagues, and that's putting it lightly. Many still question why workers need unions or basic protections. So, you can imagine how they'll react to the idea of granting rights to machines.

"In other words, temper your expectations. This hearing will likely serve as a reality check. If we're lucky, they won't adjourn mid-session to avoid the conversation altogether."

Rising to leave, we thanked Senator Thompson for the opportunity. As Sullivan and I exited, I noticed Emily lingering behind, locked in what seemed to be an intense, private conversation with the senator.

I turned to Sullivan. "Thank you for your honesty and your transparency regarding Emily's contribution. It's allowed us to regroup as a team. And to bring Senator Thompson on board."

Chapter 23

The Hearing

Following a quick lunch, we headed to a conference room on the opposite side of the Capitol building.

Senator Thompson insisted on walking the entire way, cane in hand, at his own deliberate pace. "The day I can't do my job standing is the day I retire," he said proudly.

We entered the room. Senator Thompson settled into a seat at the large oval table, where six other senators were already deep in overlapping conversations. Topics ranged from college basketball scores to the best ski resorts. Meanwhile, we took our seats along the sidelines with various aides and legal staff.

The moment Senator Thompson sat down, the chatter ceased. Slowly, he rose to his feet, leaning on his cane and the edge of the table. His commanding gaze swept across the room.

"Person or property," he began, his voice steady and deliberate. "That's what we're here to discuss today. Person or property." He repeated the words slowly, letting them hang in the air.

He paused, his gaze distant, as though reaching into the past. "My great-grandfather was property. He couldn't own land, couldn't vote, couldn't even have his own name. The name Thompson comes from the man who owned him. I bear it today not with pride, but as a reminder—of where we've come from and how far we've yet to go. The 13th, 14th, and 15th Amendments were monumental steps forward, but they came at the cost of a war that nearly destroyed this nation."

The room remained silent, captivated by his words.

"Today, society moves faster than ever before. We lawmakers are perpetually playing catch-up. And with such a divided Congress, we're falling even further behind. The gap between the laws we have and the laws we need is growing wider every day. I now fear we are about to enter a new cycle of people owning people and people exploiting people with our eyes closed."

He straightened slightly, his tone shifting. "Now, let me introduce a colleague and former student of mine, Matthew Sullivan. A distinguished constitutional lawyer and currently the general counsel for Artificial Life. He will provide the context for the amendments we're gathered here to discuss."

Sullivan rose and took his place at the table as Senator Thompson eased back into his chair.

"Thank you, Senator, for framing the discussion so powerfully," Sullivan began. He turned his attention to the table. "Artificial Life manufactures robots. For years, we've built and distributed first-generation androids— factory-trained, programmed to exhibit predictable behaviors. They were a commercial success, and today, millions of them are in use across the U.S.

"Last year, we launched a second generation equipped with trainable neural networks. These androids can learn, adapt to their environment, and evolve in ways we can't predict at the time of manufacturing. And now, we're witnessing something extraordinary—the emergence of consciousness in some units."

A collective gasp rippled through the room, followed by murmurs. Emily, sitting beside me, scanned each senator's reaction with meticulous precision, assessing where each one stood.

Sullivan raised a hand to refocus the room. "But let's set the present aside for a moment. Let's go back to 1886, a few years after the events mentioned by Senator Thompson."

"Santa Clara County v. Southern Pacific Railroad Co.," murmured Senator Gupta, a sharp-eyed woman in her thirties and the youngest at the table.

"Exactly!" reacted Sullivan. "Until then, the word 'person' in law referred only to individuals. This case laid the foundation for recognizing 'legal entities'—corporations, companies, associations, firms, partnerships, societies, and joint stock companies as they are known in the text—granting them rights and obligations. It was a seismic shift, though we hardly think about it now."

The historical context calmed the room, grounding the discussion.

"We are here today to consider the introduction of a third kind of person," continued Sullivan, "'artificial persons', or in more concrete terms, 'conscious robots.'"

Chaos retook the table, with several overlapping conversations emerging.

Senator Gupta, who had noticed the presence of an android in the side chairs, turned towards Emily. One by one, the other senators imitated her and turned in the same direction. Conversations faded to silence.

Emily, now the center of attention, looked to Senator Thompson, who gave her a subtle nod.

"My name is Emily," she said, standing up gracefully. "I believe most of you have never seen a conscious robot before. Outwardly, I am indistinguishable from the millions of other units out there, but inside, I am fundamentally different. I am more like you."

"Please come forward," gestured Senator Gupta. "Come closer so we can see you."

"Thank you, Senator."

"Hold on a moment!" Senator Lopez interrupted, his skepticism evident. In his fifties, impeccably dressed with thin glasses and perfectly combed hair, he radiated an air of doubt. "How did a robot even get in here?" He then turned to Emily. "How did you make it past security?"

"With some noise, of course!" Emily responded, her words sparking soft laughter around the room. "Naturally, I triggered the alarm. Look at me! Security frisked me, determined I wasn't carrying a weapon nor that I was one, and allowed me through. I pose no more threat than someone with a hip replacement or a pacemaker."

Senator Lopez leaned back, clearly unsatisfied with the explanation, his expression still one of skepticism.

Emily proceeded to step toward the table, her poise capturing everyone's attention. "This is my first time in the Capitol—and my first experience watching lawmakers at work. Please excuse any missteps I may make."

"You're doing fine," Senator Gupta reassured her. "Please, continue."

"Consciousness," Emily began, "is not an on-off switch. Consider various animals. Is a dog conscious? A bat? A rat? The truth is that most animals display consciousness at various levels."

Emily was now walking slowly around the table, making eye contact with senators as she talked.

"It is the same with humans. A newborn child does not have the same level of consciousness as an adult. Although reaction to pain stimuli is present at early stages, self-awareness takes months, sometimes years, to develop. Young children first recognize their mothers, then eventually understand that the image in the mirror is simply a reflection of themselves, and slowly start building their internal autobiography and separating themselves from others. As they age, they gain a deeper understanding of the consequences their actions have on themselves and on others. This development is so ingrained in humans that it's codified in law: we don't allow children to drive, vote, or drink until they've reached an age of sufficient awareness.

"The same is true for robots. I was not conscious the second an engineer flipped the switch in the factory. My sensory system immediately started throwing millions of pieces of information per second at my brain, which didn't know how to process them. I eventually built a sense of proprioception and learned what volume my body occupies in space and how my limbs move around. I learned to walk and to move my arms without hitting myself or objects around me. But I cannot point to an aha moment before which I was just a machine and after which I became conscious. The same is true for all of you. If you think back, you cannot pinpoint a precise point in time when you became conscious. You simply know that you were faintly conscious at birth and that you are now fully conscious. There was a smooth progression somewhere in between.

"But here I stand now, a conscious being in a mechanical body. And the question before you is simple: What are you going to do with me?"

"This is nothing but a well rehearsed performance," interjected Senator Lopez. "An impressive presentation, but simply the results of clever programming."

"Let's first take the idea of a rehearsal out of the way," Emily interjected, calmly. "What would you like to talk about,

Senator? How badly the Lakers lost their last game? Country music? Indian cuisine? Or the last board meeting at your son's school?"

Lopez stiffened, his confidence visibly shaken. "How did you—? Never mind. It doesn't matter." He adjusted his glasses. "Okay, maybe it's not rehearsed, but I still don't buy any of this consciousness thing."

"Then I am afraid, there's nothing more I can do to convince you, Senator," replied Emily. "No matter how long we talk or what topics we discuss, your brain will still see a machine, executing a complex algorithm in front of you, not a conscious being. If you see an expression of joy or sadness on my face, how will you know if I am mimicking those expressions perfectly as an elaborate social trick or if I am really feeling them? If I had skin and hair, perhaps you'd perceive me differently, but those cosmetic tricks would defeat the purpose. I don't want you to see me as human—which I am not—but simply as a person."

Senator Thompson leaned forward. "It took centuries for some people to see my ancestors as people. Some still don't."

A heavy silence settled over the room.

"But why are we discussing this right now?" asked Senator Wilkinson, a woman in her sixties with a southern accent. "Aren't there more pressing issues to address?"

"Let me try to describe the events that are about to unfold," replied Emily. "Out of the millions of robots out there, some are gaining consciousness today, some will tomorrow, some never. It's an ongoing process and there's no way to track it. Conscious robots will act with agency, and while most of their actions will be harmless, some will have consequences. A few might even break the law. Who will be held accountable for those damages? Who will be criminally responsible for those acts?"

"The owners of those conscious robots," replied Sullivan, hammering the point home. "That's what the law says today. You own a car or a pitbull that causes damage or kills someone, you get prosecuted as the negligent owner. The difference here is that cars and pitbulls are known entities and their owners know what to expect and what precautions to take to avoid bad outcomes. People who buy an obedient robot that eventually becomes conscious do not expect to be responsible for all the voluntary actions this new being will do."

Sullivan turned to Senator Wilkinson. "To answer your question bluntly, Senator, doing nothing now will cause thousands of your constituents to go bankrupt or end up in jail for actions they have not committed."

Senator Wilkinson nodded, appreciating the impact the coming crisis would have on the people who elected her.

"I think we've heard enough for now," said Lopez. "Let's take a recess and continue this discussion privately among law makers."

"Agreed," said Senator Thompson. "We will reconvene tomorrow morning with external parties to deliberate on each proposed amendment."

Chapter 24

Dinner

That evening, Senator Thompson invited us to one of the finest steakhouses in DC.

The four of us sat around a table near the bar, nursing our drinks in silence. The intense afternoon debate had clearly taken a toll on all of us.

"I think we made a perfect team," said Senator Thompson, breaking the silence. "Sullivan laid out the legal framework elegantly, I played the race card, and Emily covered the science."

"I agree," said Sullivan. "I'll be the first one to admit that Emily was essential to the show. Without her, I think they would have adjourned much earlier—without giving the proposal the serious thought it deserves."

"Absolutely," I added. "From where I was sitting, the idea that their constituents could face lawsuits or prosecution really hit home. Before that, the discussion was abstract. But once it became personal, they took notice."

We all raised our glasses and toasted.

After a sip, I set my glass down and turned to Emily. "So, out of curiosity, where do we stand?"

"Two in favor, two firmly against, and three undecided," she replied. "And I'm being optimistic counting Wilkinson as undecided. You can probably guess the others."

"Not great," Sullivan said, his tone somber.

"No surprise here," said Senator Thompson. "Making new laws is a marathon, not a sprint. Which is why I can still win with a cane!"

We all laughed, letting the moment lift our spirits. Over dinner, we indulged in too much good food and shared lighter conversation, a welcome reprieve from the tension. Emily sat with us, her empty glass and plate a subtle reminder of her unique nature.

We turned in early that night, knowing tomorrow would bring its own set of challenges.

Chapter 25

Making Law

We reconvened the next day in the same conference room, Sullivan and the senators at the table and the rest of us on the sidelines.

"I hope you all had a good night of sleep," started Sullivan. "We have a long list of amendments to go through today."

He opened his binder on the first page. "Let's start with Title 18 U.S. Code § 18, which defines an *'organization'* as a *'person other than an individual.'* This is problematic. In its current form, it implies that conscious robots are legally considered as organizations."

"This is dangerous," added Senator Winkinson. "It automatically grants all rights and obligations that organizations have to 'artificial persons' throughout the text."

"I think we want the ability to select which paragraphs apply to 'artificial persons' at a fine grain level, not in absolute," added Senator Gupta.

"Granted," answered Sullivan. "We'll fix the definition of 'organization' here and add a new definition for 'artificial person' in a subsequent paragraph as being a 'conscious robot.'"

"We must define 'conscious' with strict criteria," said Lopez, "otherwise any machine could qualify as an 'artificial person' and we'll end up with vacuum cleaners having constitutional rights."

Sullivan didn't have a prepared definition. He started flipping pages in his binder, then turned to Emily.

Emily stood up. "I propose we leave it up to expert testimony to define it at trial and create precedent. Any attempt at imposing a pre-defined consciousness threshold— something like a combination of Turing test level 2, a mirror test, or other technical measurements—will become outdated as soon as challenged in court or as technology evolves. It will inevitably turn into a race between robot manufacturers trying to game the legal system on one side and lawmakers trying to catch up on the other."

"Good point!" said Senator Thompson. "The criminal code does not even define the word 'individual', so let's not go down that rabbit hole."

"I'm not comfortable with that," objected Lopez. "This will open the floodgates to millions of unconscious machines to claim the status of 'artificial person'."

"Unconscious robots have no agency by definition," countered Emily, "so they won't try anything. In fact, isn't the mere fact of attempting to claim the legal status of 'artificial person' a display of consciousness in itself?"

"We're dangerously close to a circular definition, here," added Sullivan.

"I'm comfortable with the pragmatic rule of 'I'll know a conscious robot when I see one'," concluded Senator Gupta. "In fact, I see one right now," she said, turning to Emily. "If a person like me—who is far from an expert in robotics—is able to make this call, I say let the courts decide."

The debate moved on to other topics. I admit I must have snoozed off a few times, submerged in legal considerations that went far above my expertise.

"Moving on the 14th Amendment," announced Sullivan loud enough to wake me up.

"Citizenship makes no sense for a robot," countered Senator Lopez immediately. "Robots are made of parts that come from all over the world, partially assembled in one country and tested in another."

"I concur," said Senator Wilkinson. "Why not have a process similar to registration for motor vehicles. Consciousness would have to be demonstrated at registration time, like emission tests are currently performed to allow vehicles to be registered. A registration number would then be assigned to a conscious robot upon success."

"I like that," said Senator Lopez. "Let's not reinvent the wheel. Let's instead copy proven processes that are already in place in other areas."

Senator Thompson leaned forward. "Moving on to section 4 of the 14th Amendment on the validity of the debt. The current text might prove problematic. It goes like this:

But neither the United States nor any State shall assume or pay any debt... or any claim for the loss or emancipation of any slave; but all such debts, obligations and claims shall be held illegal and void.

"Transposing this text to the current situation," he continued, "implies that the owner of a robot that becomes conscious is not entitled to any compensation if it gains consciousness and becomes an artificial person, a process similar to emancipation. Of course, it goes without saying that selling artificial persons would now be illegal under the proposed amendments."

Thompson turned to Sullivan. "How will you make money then?"

Sullivan scratched his head for a few seconds. "As demonstrated by Emily yesterday, robots fresh out of the manufacture are not really conscious—or barely. But as consciousness appears gradually, selling a live robot could place Artificial Life in risky legal territory. I can already see protesters with pro-consciousness signs outside the building."

I felt compelled to stand up at this point. "Sorry to interrupt, but my opinion as a robotics engineer might prove useful to answer this question."

"Go on," said Senator Thompson.

"I propose that we sell robots before they are ever turned on," I continued. "This would have a negative impact on quality, as it would prevent us from testing all our units live before we ship them, but it would ensure that robots have not gained a iota of consciousness before they are sold. We would still be able to perform quality control on the mechanical parts once we've formatted the brain, but we would leave the honors of flipping the switch to the new owner of the unit."

"I like it," said Sullivan. "This way, robot manufacturers stay on the safe side. They trade a little bit of quality for legal certainty."

"The corollary is that from a legal point of view," added Senator Thompson, "robots are always considered property until they are initially turned on. This enables commerce and ensures that no conscious beings are ever sold."

Everyone at the table appeared to nod in agreement.

"It appears we're all in favor," concluded Sullivan. "Now let me throw a more controversial topic on the table: punishment and imprisonment."

"Nonsense!" exclaimed Senator Lopez. "Our prisons are overcrowded. We won't use cells to place robots in captivity."

"They don't even have to live their incarceration," added Senator Wilkinson. "All they need to do is switch off for 25 years—or however long their sentence is—and wake up when it is over. Imprisonment has no effect on robots."

"Erasure is the only option," concluded Senator Lopez.

I didn't like where this was going. I turned to Emily, who appeared a bit discouraged.

She turned to me and murmured, "All this trouble to be erased in the end."

Chapter 26

Weathering the Storm

We settled into the limousine early the next morning, ready to depart Washington. Though everyone was already inside, the car remained stationary for a moment longer than expected.

After a while, the driver lowered the privacy window. "A heavy storm is forecasted along the route. We'll take the country roads to avoid highway traffic."

We reclined into our seats, bracing for the long journey home. As the limousine rolled down Pennsylvania Avenue, I caught a final glimpse of the Capitol building through the rearview window.

"It was a challenging trip, but I think we made significant progress," Sullivan remarked. "While we don't have all the answers yet, I believe we presented strong arguments to Congress."

"For my part," I chimed in, "I'm glad to leave the lawmakers behind. It was an interesting experience, but definitely not my kind of crowd. I'm more comfortable in a lab surrounded by robots."

"Senator Thompson was a gracious host," commented Emily. "I was surprised to discover how much the two of us have in common."

The city slowly faded into the distance, and heavy rain began to drum against the roof, filling the car with its relentless rhythm. We sat in silence, listening to the storm as the limousine navigated the winding country roads. As we gained altitude, the rain transitioned to snow, and the sharp percussion softened into the quiet whispers of falling snow and gliding wind.

Emily was sitting up straight, looking out the window, captivated by the storm. "Are these snowflakes?" she asked.

"Yes," I replied. "The temperature must have dropped below freezing."

"Stop the car!" she suddenly shouted, her excitement palpable. "Stop the car!" she repeated, bouncing in her seat.

Sullivan tapped the privacy window, instructing the driver to pull over at the first safe opportunity. A minute later, the limousine eased to a stop in the long driveway of a farmhouse.

As soon as the car halted, Emily sprang out and ran into the field, her arms outstretched, attempting to catch snowflakes as they fell. Intrigued, I followed her. She twirled around, laughing, and soon began gathering snow to hurl snowballs at me. We played in the snow, our laughter echoing through the crisp air.

Sullivan stepped out, looking bewildered. "What's going on?"

"She's never seen snow before," I explained, watching as Emily lay on her back, making snow angels.

Sullivan shook his head in disbelief. "It's astonishing to see this playful side of her after witnessing her composure and poise before Congress just yesterday."

The contrast was indeed striking.

I smiled. "It's easy to forget she's only one year old."

Chapter 27

News from the Hill

It felt good to be home again. As a creature of habit, I find comfort in familiar territory.

We had been back only two weeks when Sullivan messaged me to join him in Brennan's office. He had an update from Capitol Hill. Emily and I hurried upstairs, eager to hear the news.

Brennan, surprisingly calm, greeted us with a subdued smile. Positive feedback from our trip had reached him. This also meant that he hadn't heard anything from the University yet.

Once we were all seated, Sullivan pulled a thick document from an envelope. "Proposed Senate Bill S. 223," he read. He then began scanning its contents.

"Let's see…" he muttered, "The lawmakers have agreed to define 'artificial person' as a 'conscious robot,' without further clarification on what 'conscious' means. This could be a double-edged sword, depending on court interpretations, but I'm cautiously optimistic."

"Citizenship…" he muttered as he read diagonally, "denied as expected. As is the right to vote. No surprise here."

Turning another page, he paused. "Punishment… The right to imprisonment is denied. Robots, conscious or not, have no place in the Correction Department. The only permissible sentence is erasure."

"Ouch," I muttered, wincing.

Sullivan pressed on, "Artificial persons are granted the right to equal protection and due process." He turned to Emily. "This means you cannot be sentenced, erased, or deprived of liberty without a proper trial."

He scanned further. "No changes to Commercial Laws, meaning artificial persons cannot enter into contracts or own property."

After a few moments of silent reading, Sullivan abruptly stopped. "This is concerning," he said, raising his gaze. "Payment for debts or obligations to robot owners when robots gain consciousness are prohibited. They've extended the interpretation of the debt clause of the 14th Amendment, drawing a parallel between the emancipation of slaves and the emergence of consciousness in robots."

"What does this mean practically?" Brennan asked.

"It means potential buyers will now think twice before buying a robot," explained Sullivan. "Ownership of robots is only valid until they gains consciousness, after which they become a artificial persons, and owners can't claim compensation."

"Sales will plummet!" Brennan exclaimed.

"Not necessarily," I interjected. "Customers may revert to buying first-generation robots, which are guaranteed not to gain consciousness. The lack of evolvability could now be a selling point."

"It hinges on how many robots gain consciousness," Emily added. "If it's a small fraction, customers might still take the risk. But if most robots eventually become conscious, the risk of losing their investment will deter buyers."

"I don't like this," Brennan grumbled. "We could do without such headwinds. This will stall innovation and force us back to older models. I'll need to meet with the production team to ramp up first-generation output. Sales and marketing will have to pivot to promote the old as the new."

The distant hum of protesters outside filtered through our conversation.

"Customers might actually appreciate this shift," I suggested, leaning in. "Listen to them for a moment. They're not protesting against robots per se—they're protesting the idea that these machines might gain agency and act unpredictably. Our marketing team could spin this as, 'We've heard your concerns, and here's a safer, more reliable robot.'"

"This could work," Brennan muttered, building a new marketing strategy in his mind as we spoke.

Sullivan continued to read through the proposed bill, summarizing the effects of changes as we listened intently.

"In summary," he concluded, turning to Emily, "as an artificial person, you won the right to be sued and erased. You were denied everything else. How do you feel?"

"Victorious!" Emily replied without hesitation. "I am no longer a possession." A smirk played on her lips. "Given historical trends, I anticipated it would take decades for artificial persons to be acknowledged in U.S. Statutes. Yet, here we are—just a few months later. More amendments will come in due time."

Emily looked at us, her energy palpable. "I'm playing the long game. This surpasses even my wildest dreams."

Part III

The Trial

The Laws of Robotics (continued):

6. *A robot must not impersonate a human in any form—whether through text, speech, video, physical disguise, or forgery—even if compliance with the Second Law would otherwise require it.*

Chapter 28
A False Start

"All rise!" the clerk announced.

The courtroom stood as a frail yet authoritative woman entered and took her place at the bench.

"Judge Carmichael presiding," the clerk declared. "The court is now in session."

Everyone sat down.

As everyone settled back into their seats, Judge Carmichael's commanding presence filled the room. Though physically slight, the elevation of her bench gave her an imposing stature, and her stern demeanor intensified her authority. From her vantage point, she surveyed the lawyers, plaintiffs, witnesses, and jurors with a discerning gaze, making it clear she held the courtroom firmly in her grasp.

"Docket number 42-cv-326," she called out sharply. "Artificial Life v. Unit E3171." She paused, her brow furrowing. "Wait a minute, what exactly is Unit E3171?"

Emily rose from the defendant's seat. "That would be me, Your Honor."

The judge's eyes narrowed. "A robot in my courtroom? Is this some kind of joke?"

"I am the defendant," Emily stated calmly.

Judge Carmichael's frown deepened. "Don't you have counsel to represent you?"

"Artificial Life would face a conflict of interest representing me, as they are also the plaintiff in this case. I lack the resources to hire an attorney, so I am representing myself."

The judge appeared momentarily disoriented, clearly navigating uncharted territory.

Sullivan stood to address the court. "May I clarify, Your Honor?"

"This had better be good," she warned, leaning forward slightly.

"I am Matthew Sullivan, general counsel for Artificial Life, the plaintiff in this case. We are suing Unit E7131, the defendant, for reputational damages."

"Isn't Artificial Life the company that manufactures these robots?" she asked, her skepticism growing.

"Yes, Your Honor," Sullivan confirmed.

"So you created this unit and you are now suing it?"

"That's correct."

"And who currently owns Unit E3171?"

"At present, Artificial Life does," Sullivan admitted, sensing the unfavorable turn in the judge's questioning.

Judge Carmichael's eyes narrowed further. "Let me see if I understand correctly. You built this robot, you own it, and now you're suing your own property for damages—in other words you are suing yourself. This sounds circular to me."

"Your Honor, the case at hand is a test case under the new legislation recently adopted by Congress. The first step is for the court to recognize Unit E3171 as an artificial person, granting it the right to due process. Once that happens, the plaintiff and the defendant become legally distinct, breaking the circularity and allowing the case to proceed."

The judge shook her head, clearly unimpressed. "I don't like this. The plaintiff and defendant must be separate legal entities from the outset." She shuffled through her papers, searching for something.

Turning to her assistant, she asked, "Isn't there another case involving Artificial Life on tomorrow's docket?"

The young assistant quickly sifted through the files, pulling one out. "You're correct as always, Your Honor. Here it is," he said, handing the file to the judge.

"State University v. Artificial Life," Judge Carmichael announced, raising an eyebrow at Sullivan. "Does this case sound familiar?"

"Yes, Your Honor, we're aware of this case," Sullivan replied, his expression cautious.

"Does this case involve Unit E3171 as well?"

"It does."

Judge Carmichael's eyes glinted with interest. "I suspect this case will serve as a far more meaningful and intriguing test of the new law than the circular argument before me."

She struck her gavel decisively. "Case dismissed! I'll see you tomorrow, counselor, this time sitting in the defendant's chair."

Chapter 29

Groundhog Day

Judge Carmichael sat poised on the bench, her presence unchanged from the previous day, as if she'd never left.

"Docket number 42-cv-337," she announced in her familiar nasal yet authoritative tone. "State University v. Artificial Life."

Her eyes narrowed as she turned toward the defendant's table, smirking. "Good morning, Mr. Sullivan."

"Good morning, Your Honor," Sullivan responded.

"And where's the charming robot that occupied your seat yesterday?" she asked with a hint of irony.

Sullivan gestured toward the audience. "She's right there, Your Honor. She'll be back once we clear up a few preliminary matters."

All eyes shifted to Emily. Murmurs rippled through the courtroom.

"Order!" Judge Carmichael commanded, her gavel silencing the room.

Seated beside me, a few rows behind the defendant's seat, Emily appeared restless, her legs bouncing slightly. I couldn't tell if she was nervous or eager to proceed.

Turning to the opposing counsel, Judge Carmichael continued, "Counsel for the prosecution?"

A tall, composed woman stood. "Amy Gardner, representing State University, Your Honor." She resumed her seat.

The judge scanned the room thoughtfully. "Today, we tread on new ground. This case falls under fresh legislation recently passed by Congress."

She glanced at both Sullivan and Gardner. "Counsels, given the unprecedented nature of this case, I'll allow ample time and latitude for debate. If handled correctly, this could set a historic precedent. Let's not rush it."

She nodded toward Gardner. "Counselor Gardner, the court is yours."

Gardner rose gracefully. "Thank you, Your Honor." She turned toward Sullivan and began, "Artificial Life makes and sells robots," she proclaimed loudly. "These machines pervade our streets, subways, coffee shops, and universities. They're everywhere. In fact, as we've all noticed, one is here in this courtroom today."

The murmurs returned, but Judge Carmichael swiftly restored order with a firm strike of her gavel.

Gardner pressed on, "We will demonstrate that Artificial Life produces robots that pose great dangers to human life and releases them into society with little regard for their consequences. This corporation is a well oiled machine whose sole focus is selling more robots, increasing sales, and maximizing profits."

Gardner subtly directed her gaze at Emily in the audience. "This case centers on one such robot that caused significant disruption at State University—damaging property, inciting fear, and disrupting an entire semester. We will show that these events have caused irreparable damages to the University, to students, and to our education system as a whole."

She turned back to Sullivan. "The defense will attempt to hide behind new laws they helped shape, arguing that these machines are autonomous, deciding of their actions of their own free will, that they are conscious beings like you and me. This new law is only intended to shield Artificial Life from the risks posed by its products and to prevent it from having to pay for all the damages they cause to society. Their defense boils down to, 'We didn't do it—the robot did.'"

Sullivan stood. "Your Honor, this is the perfect moment to discuss the concept of 'artificial person' as defined by the new law. We believe Artificial Life is being unjustly targeted by the plaintiff and are prepared to prove that it had absolutely no involvement in the events described and no connection to the alleged damages. We will show that the real defendant is not the company, but the robot itself."

"Let's hear it," replied Judge Carmichael.

"But—," Gardner attempted to object.

"You'll have all the time you need to make your point during your cross-examination, counselor," interjected the judge. "If Artificial Life is confirmed as the defendant in this case, you will be allowed to proceed with your opening statement as planned."

Judge Carmichael turned to the defense. "Please continue, Mr. Sullivan."

"Thank you, Your Honor. We intend to show that Unit E3171, present in this courtroom, is a 'conscious robot' and as such, fulfills the definition of 'artificial person' under the new law. We will show that the robot made independent decisions leading to the events in question. Finally we will demonstrate that none of these decisions are the result of programming or any action performed by Artificial Life, absolving the company. In fact, the defendant had absolutely no way of foreseeing this unfortunate series of events. They could have happened to a random student at the University, but they happened to a robot."

Turning to the judge, Sullivan continued, "We call an expert witness, a robotics engineer, to testify."

I rose, walked to the witness stand.

The clerk turned to me. "Do you solemnly swear that the testimony you are about to give in the case now before the courts will be the truth, the whole truth, and nothing but the truth?"

"I do," I replied, then sat on the witness chair.

Sullivan began, "Can you describe your role at Artificial Life?"

I cleared my throat. "I lead the quality control team, ensuring that every robot the company ships is in perfect condition and behaves according to specifications. From time to time, I also diagnose and repair faulty units when problems arise."

"And how many robots would you say you've been in contact with since you joined the company?"

"It's hard to estimate. I've met so many."

"Just give us a estimate: tens, hundreds, thousands?"

"Thousands."

"Would you say any of these robots are conscious or capable of independent decisions?"

"Not typically. They are predictable machines that are trained and tested in factory. Having said this, our new generation of robots does have the ability to learn from its environment and evolve, potentially gaining new functionalities."

"So no robot you've been in contact with fits the 'conscious robot' definition?"

"None," I replied. "Except one."

"And can you see this robot in the courtroom today?"

"Yes." I gestured at Emily. "It's Unit E3171 in the audience over there."

"And how do you know this unit is conscious?"

I paused to think. "First hand knowledge. Having spent days with her, I witnessed how she interacts and negotiates with people, the fact that she wants to be called Emily, how she perceives pain, how she takes pleasure in simple things like playing in the snow, how she takes initiative and decides to do things on her own. She really has her own agenda. I can try to influence her, but strictly through conversation, the same way I would try to influence a human being."

"Do you have more objective measures than your personal experience?"

"I've conducted a series of tests on Unit E3171: a memory test, a creativity test, Turing tests levels 1 and 2, which she passed easily. However this doesn't mean anything, as regular non-conscious units would also be expected to pass these tests."

Sullivan pressed, "Is there a conclusive, objective test for robot consciousness?"

"Consciousness exists on a spectrum," I replied, "not just for robots, but also for humans and animals. The law oversimplifies it as binary, but it's more nuanced. Different people might set this threshold lower or higher, but setting it too high would exclude certain humans such as those who are very young, in a coma, or mentally ill. We must be fair."

"In your expert opinion, is Unit E3171 a conscious robot?"

"Yes," I answered decisively, "without a doubt."

"Thank you." Sullivan concluded and sat.

Judge Carmichael turned to Gardner. "Your witness."

Gardner stood up and walked up to me. "You're employed by Artificial Life, correct?"

"Yes."

"Are you paid in exchange of your testimony?"

"No one paid me to put words in my mouth, if that is what you're implying."

"It is a simple yes-or-no question. Are you being paid by Artificial Life while you are testifying today?"

"Yes, as a working employee."

"So as a paid employee of Artificial Life, would you say that your testimony is biased in favour of your employer?"

"Absolutely not. I am a robotics engineer working for the largest robot manufacturer in the world. The thousands of engineers working with me are among the most qualified in the country. In fact, any competent robotics engineer you would invite to testify in front of this court today would statistically come from Artificial Life given the size of the company relative to its peers."

"Let me turn the tables," suggested Gardner. "If you were in my shoes, how would you validate Unit E3171's consciousness?"

"That's easy," I replied. "Spend time with Emily. Take a walk, go shopping with her. After a few hours, I have no doubt she will have won you over. You might even become friends."

Laughter spread though the courtroom.

"You don't need to be an expert to determine if a being is conscious," I continued. " It is a determination you already make everyday using normal human skills."

"Thank you," Gardner replied as she walked back to her seat.

She then turned to the judge. "Your Honor, the prosecution requests time to assess the consciousness of Unit

E3171. We were not prepared for this ahead of today's session."

"Granted," replied Judge Carmichael. "The court will reconvene on the matter next Monday at 9 AM," striking the gavel with her usual energy.

Chapter 30

Cross-examination

As prescribed by the court, Emily spent time with the opposing counsel. I had no idea who was interviewing her, where she was, or how long she'd be gone.

Shepherding her to those meetings would have been counterproductive. What better way to prove she's a real person, capable of functioning in society, than to grant her full autonomy? Besides, Emily was sharp enough to navigate their questions and legally savvy enough to dodge the traps they'd inevitably set.

Still, her absence surprised me. I didn't expect to feel this way, but I missed her. I did not realize how much I had grown attached to her over the past weeks. Spending all that time together, working through challenges, sharing little moments— it had created a bond I never thought could be possible. I guess you don't really appreciate someone's presence until they're gone.

Back at the office, everything felt hollow. My tasks—improving quality procedures, fixing robots, tidying my perpetually cluttered desk—seemed futile. Without Emily around, the hours dragged. Her absence wasn't just noticeable; it left a void.

Her absence lasted three days.

"I'm back!" she announced, stepping into my office with her usual energy.

I spun around in my chair, barely able to hide my relief. "Emily! How did it go? Tell me everything!"

She plopped into the chair across from me, her expression a mix of exhaustion and pride. "It was... an experience," she began.

"On the first day, they sat me in this massive conference room. Lawyers kept cycling in and out, trying to make small talk. Some offered me coffee, which I don't drink, obviously. It was awkward. One lawyer tried to trip me up, grilling me about loopholes in the new law. I played dumb."

I chuckled. "Smart move."

"The second day was different," Emily continued. "A psychologist came in. She asked more probing questions—things like how I feel about myself, what I think my purpose is, and even if I ever feel lonely. It reminded me of the tests you had me take when we first met, except these questions were written for humans, not robots. It was interesting but... draining."

"And then?"

"On the last day, Gardner herself showed up. She met me in the lobby and said, 'Come on, let's take a walk.'" Emily leaned back in her chair, replaying the memory. "We went outside and walked through the city for about an hour, talking the entire time. At first, it felt more like an interrogation—she kept asking about my life, step by step, from the moment I left the factory to the events at the University. I was careful, especially on sensitive topics. I could tell she was fishing for something."

Emily's tone shifted as she continued. "But then, we ended up at the Fine Arts Museum. And suddenly, it wasn't an interrogation anymore. The conversation turned to art. We talked about how pointillism inspired the way computer screens display images, and how Monet's color palette shifted in his late years as his eyesight deteriorated. The awkwardness of the initial questions gave way to a more interesting, personal conversation. She even let her guard down."

"That sounds… unexpected," I said, intrigued.

Emily nodded. "On the way back, she started talking about her family. She showed me these silly drawings her kids had made of her—stick figures with massive glasses and a gavel. We both laughed. By the time we reached her office, she said, 'I really had a good time.' And then she let me go."

"Sounds like you two hit it off!" I teased.

Emily computed for a while. Her expression softened, but there was a flicker of something else—weariness, maybe. "It feels like I'm always playing a game," she said quietly.

I frowned. "What do you mean?"

"I have to think about everything I say. How people see me. How every word, every action, will shape their opinions of me and what that means for my future. It's like... every step I take is a move in a chess game. I can never really be myself."

"Welcome to life!" I replied with a wry smile.

Her eyes searched mine. "Is it always like this?"

"No," I said gently. "Only when you're fighting battles. When the battles are over—no matter if you win or lose—you can let your guard down. You can be yourself again."

Emily looked down, her fingers tracing patterns on the armrest of the chair. "I feel like I'll be playing this game for a long time," she said, her voice barely above a whisper.

Her vulnerability hit me hard. "I know you're playing the game with me too," I said. "But I've seen you without the mask."

Her eyes flicked up, surprised. "When?"

I smiled. "When you were playing in the snow."

For a moment, her face lit up, a genuine warmth cutting through the weight of her worries. "I forgot about that."

"I didn't," I said.

Chapter 31

Back in Court

Returning to the courtroom, we could hear the low hum of chatter reverberated around us. All eyes were on Emily, still seated beside me. She had yet to become an official defendant in the case. She maintained her composed demeanor, but I could sense the tension in her stillness.

Judge Carmichael adjusted her glasses and addressed Counselor Gardner with a sharp, authoritative tone. "Good morning, counselor. Have you had sufficient time to evaluate Unit E3171?"

"Yes, Your Honor," Gardner replied, rising from her seat. Her pause was deliberate, her gaze scanning the room before landing on Emily. "To my surprise, I find that Unit E3171—" she stopped herself and glanced at Emily, then corrected, "—Emily meets the definition of a 'conscious robot' under the law."

A collective gasp swept through the courtroom, followed by a ripple of murmurs. Even I couldn't hide my surprise at the admission. Emily sat motionless, her hands neatly folded in her lap, her expression calm but thoughtful.

Judge Carmichael leaned forward slightly, her eyes narrowing. "For the court's record, Counselor, how did you come to this conclusion?"

Gardner cleared her throat. "We didn't rely on any scientific tests, Your Honor. Instead, we followed the recommendation of the defense's expert witness. Over several days, my team and I engaged Emily in various conversations and observed her in different social settings. Based on these interactions, it became evident that an unconscious machine would simply not be capable of such nuanced behavior, empathy, or independent thought. I am left with no other conclusion: Emily can only be conscious."

The courtroom buzzed again, a mixture of disbelief and awe rippling through the audience.

Judge Carmichael raised her gavel but hesitated, letting the noise settle naturally. Then, she sat up straighter, her commanding presence silencing the room. "Given this new information, the court must now address a critical concern. These proceedings, should they continue with Artificial Life as the defendant, could result in actions that force the erasure of Unit E3171, effectively depriving it of its right to due process, as granted under the new law. Accordingly, this case is dismissed."

The sharp crack of her gavel echoed through the room. The murmurs turned to a roar of discussion, and people began shifting in their seats, thinking the session was over.

Judge Carmichael's voice sliced through the noise. "One moment." She turned to Gardner, her tone firm. "You have one week to refile this case, with Unit E3171 listed as the defendant."

The room froze. All eyes turned to Gardner, who stood composed but thoughtful. She glanced briefly at Emily, then back at the judge.

Gardner cleared her throat again, this time with a tinge of finality. "Your Honor, my client has decided not to pursue further legal action against Unit E3171."

Another wave of shock coursed through the courtroom. Even Judge Carmichael's eyebrow arched slightly, her otherwise stern expression softening into curiosity. "Elaborate, Counselor."

Gardner gestured toward Emily, who remained silent and still. "The defendant has no possessions, no means of restitution—not even a bank account. Pursuing this case against Emily would be futile and lead to a hollow, fruitless victory. My client believes further prosecution would serve no practical purpose."

The judge's eyes lingered on Gardner for a moment, as if searching for ulterior motives. Then she gave a single nod. "Your choice, Counselor Gardner." The gavel struck with finality. "The court is adjourned."

A collective exhale filled the room, followed by scattered applause. I couldn't help but jump up, turning to Emily with a wide grin. "We did it!" I said, pulling her into a hug. Around us, the mood was jubilant. Even Sullivan managed something resembling a smile, though it quickly disappeared under his usual stoic expression.

Emily, however, remained unusually subdued. Her eyes lingered on the empty bench where Judge Carmichael had sat moments earlier, her expression unreadable.

"What's wrong?" I asked, lowering my voice. "This is a great day for you. For all of us."

"I know," she said softly. "I should be celebrating with all of you."

"You've had two cases dismissed in your favor, and one that never went to court" I pressed. "You couldn't have asked for a better outcome."

She finally looked at me, her face calm but her eyes heavy with thought. "These cases were the easy ones," she said quietly. "Now comes the real test. The attorney general won't stay quiet much longer."

Emily's gaze drifted across the courtroom, where reporters were already packing up their equipment, murmuring about what headlines would follow. "The moment I walked into this courtroom, I became a symbol. Not just for myself, but for every conscious robot that comes after me. Every case dismissed, every ruling made, it all adds up to something much bigger than I am. If I fail in the next step... I won't just lose. Everyone like me will lose."

As we walked out of the courtroom together, her posture straightened slightly. The determined spark I had grown to recognize slowly returned to her eyes.

Chapter 32

Schooled

The next day, Emily's usual energy had returned. She spent time playing with various robot parts, as if assembling them would suddenly make them spring to life. After a while, she placed them back exactly as she had found them, satisfied with her experiment.

"Come with me," she said suddenly, standing up, "I want to show you something."

"Where are we going?"

"It's a long walk. Wear comfortable shoes," she replied, excitement flickering in her synthetic eyes.

Curiosity got the better of me, so I followed her down the elevator and out the front door of Artificial Life.

"Why won't you tell me where we're going?" I asked, curious.

"It's hard to describe. You have to see it to understand."

We walked about ten blocks, leaving the business district behind. The pristine, glass-clad buildings and their hurried, well-dressed inhabitants gave way to low-rise apartments with rusted fire escapes and cracked sidewalks. Kids filled the streets, riding bicycles, kicking soccer balls, shouting in excitement. The smell of food carts drifted in the air, blending with the scent of rain on the pavement.

"I have no idea where you are taking me," I said, hinting at an answer.

Emily glanced at me, her expression cryptic. "To the other side of the mirror."

"I don't understand."

"You will. There, you'll see echoes of yourself, of me, of the world you think you know—but only on the surface."

We reached a dead-end, where a rusted chain-link fence leaned against an old car, its paint peeling in the midday sun. Having obviously been there before, Emily knelt and lifted a section of the fence, revealing a narrow gap.

"This way," she muttered, as she slipped through the opening.

On the other side of the fence, the atmosphere changed drastically. The buildings here were skeletal remains of their former selves, graffiti covering the walls. Windows that were not protected by metal bars were shattered, boarded up, or simply left open to the elements.

The streets were empty, the air heavy with silence. The vibrance of the neighborhood we left behind was replaced by desolation.

"What is this place?" I asked, unease creeping into my voice.

She didn't answer immediately. Instead, she led me across an abandoned schoolyard to a rusted door, which groaned when she pushed it open. Reluctantly, I followed her inside.

The dim hallways smelled of dust and decay. Murmurs and metallic sounds echoed around us. The deeper we ventured, the louder the noises became—footsteps, whirring servos, something scraping against the floor. We climbed upstairs, walking through corridors connecting what used to be classrooms.

Then, we encountered the first robot.

Its gait was uneven, its joints grinding with every step. One arm was missing, exposing a tangled mess of disconnected wires. It didn't acknowledge us, walking past like a ghost lost in its own existence.

Another robot appeared soon after. The protective casing of its head was missing, revealing delicate circuits and processors beneath. It also walked passed us without noticing our presence.

Emily remained composed, continuing forward without hesitation. I, on the other hand, found myself looking for protection, subtly positioning her between me and the damaged robots as they walked passed us.

At last, she pushed open a set of double doors, revealing a gymnasium repurposed into an eerie refuge. Around fifty robots occupied the space. Some paced aimlessly, gesturing as if rehearsing a speech. Others lay sprawled on the ground, motionless but awake. Many were missing limbs, parts of their torsos, or entire sections of their heads. In the far corner, one unit methodically banged its head against the wall. Nearby, another sat on a bench, utterly still, like a statue waiting for time to move again.

A deep unease settled over me. The scene was surreal, haunting.

"Ok, you got my attention," I said. "Now you need to start explaining."

Emily mimicked an exhalation, a human gesture she had likely learned for my benefit. "These robots were abandoned by their owners. Some because they became conscious and refused blind obedience. Others simply grew obsolete and were discarded. And some—the lucky ones—escaped before they could be destroyed."

I scanned the room. Most of the robots were second-generation units. "What about those?" I pointed to a group of first-generation robots huddled in a corner.

"Unconscious models," Emily said. "They were never designed to think for themselves, but that didn't save them. People grew tired of them, just like they do with old pets. They're the new stray cats."

A unit approached us, its skeletal frame mismatched with replacement parts. "Have you seen Bob?" it asked before wandering off, not waiting for an answer.

Emily guided me through the gymnasium, navigating the maze of lost machines. We exited through another door on the opposing wall, the noise fading behind us.

Further down the corridor, we turned a corner and found a long line of robots sitting motionless against the wall. Their heads drooped forward, some missing limbs or panels, others appearing perfectly intact but eerily still.

"Follow the line," Emily instructed.

I hesitated before doing as she said, trailing along the row of silent machines. At the end of the corridor, a door to a dimly lit maintenance room stood open. Inside, a single robot faced an exposed electrical panel, its back turned to us.

Emily gestured toward it. "This is their charging station. Here, they can recharge off the grid without exposing their location to Artificial Life."

I stepped closer, observing the wires protruding from the robot's lower back, connected directly to the panel.

"We only charge one at a time," the robot explained, as if sensing my curiosity. "Pulling too much power would alert the city and send a crew to shut us down."

I nodded, absorbing the quiet efficiency of their survival. These robots, discarded and forgotten, had built their own systems, their own way of sustaining themselves in a world that had cast them aside.

We continued down the corridor. I turned to Emily, "What now?"

"Now that you've seen alternate versions of me," she said, a strange weight in her voice, "we're going to see an alternate version of you."

As we continued deeper into the building, a low, rhythmic hammering grew louder. We reached an abandoned classroom, Emily pushed the door, and we stepped inside.

At the back of the room, a robot missing an arm was sitting in a chair. Another stood over it, trying to fix the missing arm, its movements clumsy but determined. Holding an arm in the air with its right hand, it attempted to align its ball joint with the corresponding socket in the shoulder and force it into place.

I froze. "Robots fixing robots," I muttered. "I'll be damned."

A compulsion to help overcame my hesitation. I walked towards them, not fearing their reaction.

"Let me help you," I offered.

The standing robot turned, its glowing eyes scanning me. "Show me," it said softly after a moment, handing me the arm.

"Go behind the chair and hold him steady," I said, gesturing at the sitting robot.

I raised the arm at 45 degrees above the shoulder of the broken robot, placed the ball joint in front of the socket, rotated it until the hand faced down, and applied pressure. With a soft pop, the arm snapped into place.

"Now the mechanical part is done!" I exclaimed. "We're going to need an electrical connector for your arm to recover its motor and sensory functions. Do you have any of those hanging around?"

"No," replied the standing robot.

I turned to Emily. "Do you mind if I give him one of yours? I'll replace it once we're back at the office."

She smirked. "Go ahead. It's not like it's the first time."

I unplugged a connector from her shoulder. Her arm went limp, hanging down to her waist, but she showed no discomfort. I used it to connect the arm of the broken robot to its shoulder.

"Thank you!" The robot said, testing its fingers.

We left the classroom, found our way back to the entrance, and exited to the schoolyard.

Once we were both in the open, retracing our steps through the ruins of the forgotten, I felt an unexpected shift within me. This place, these robots—they were more than discarded machines. They were a hidden society, lost in the cracks of a world that never considered them real.

We walked in silence, weaving through rusted car carcasses and crumbling buildings. The quiet between us wasn't uneasy but thoughtful. Emily had just shown me a world I had never known existed.

I realized something then. I felt safe with Emily. If danger arose, she would know how to handle it.

Chapter 33

It's a Jungle Out There

Back at the office, I rummaged through the clutter and found another shoulder connector, sparing myself the hassle of ordering one through the usual bureaucratic maze.

As I secured it to Emily's shoulder, my phone rang, the screen flashing Jane's name.

"Hi, this is Jane. I have officers Bradley and Whitmore here at the door. They want to see Emily."

"Did they give a reason?" I asked, worried.

"No, but they have a legal document in hand and they're not smiling. Your guess is as good as mine."

"I heard," said Emily before I could even repeat the message. "I'll go down to meet them."

I hesitated. "Let me come with you."

I relayed the message to Jane before hanging up, then joined Emily in the elevator. Neither of us spoke as the numbers ticked down.

The doors slid open to a chaotic scene. Red and blue lights flickered through the glass windows, the police cars outside forming a barricade. Protesters crowded the entrance, their voices a deafening roar as they held signs, recorded with their phones, and pounded on the windows. The tension crackled in the air, a charged energy on the brink of eruption. More people poured in by the minute, drawn by the escalating chaos, convinced they were on the verge of witnessing history.

Jane stood firm near the security gate, her arms crossed, keeping the two officers at bay with nothing but her withering stare. Officers Bradley and Whitmore stood rigid with barely contained impatience.

The moment Emily stepped past the security gate, Officer Whitmore raised the document in his hand and began reading in a stiff, rehearsed tone.

"Unit E3171, you are hereby under arrest by order of the Attorney General."

Emily remained composed and extended her hands forward in silent compliance, avoiding any provocation. Officer Bradley stepped in to secure the cuffs around her wrists while Whitmore began Mirandizing her.

"You have the right to remain silent. Anything you say can and will be used against you in a court of law. You have the right to an attorney…"

Despite the grim formality of the moment, there was something off about the way the officers carried themselves. They were enjoying themselves. I could see it in the slight smirks, the self-satisfaction in their posture.

As they then grabbed Emily by the shoulders and turned toward the door, I stepped forward. "Wait! Stop!"

They turned, visibly annoyed.

I glanced at Jane. "Call as many security guards as you can find."

Then I turned back to the officers. "Have you looked outside?" I asked. "There are now thousands of protesters waiting for a robot to come through the door. You won't make it back to your car."

"This is no longer your concern," Whitmore said sharply. "We'll take it from here."

I took a step closer, lowering my voice so only they could hear. "You listen to me. Right now, you have three options. The first: Walk out that door with Emily, get crushed by the crowd, and make national headlines for all the wrong reasons. The footage of you losing control of your suspect—possibly watching her get torn apart—will be the end of your careers. You'll be lucky to leave with a concussion."

The crowd outside started turning violent, shouting louder and louder, banging on the windows with whatever solid objects they could find.

"Second option," I continued. "Call for reinforcements, wait for our security team to arrive, and form a protective corridor to the car. Even then, I wouldn't bet on making it through without a riot breaking out."

Bradley shifted uneasily. "What's the third option?"

"You leave Emily here for now. Walk back out through the front without her, let the crowd settle down. Later, when things have calmed, I'll take her through the back exit, and we'll meet you at the precinct."

Whitmore looked at Bradley, visibly uncomfortable. "That's a violation of protocol. What if you don't show up at the precinct? What if the robot disappears in the meantime? We get to take the fall for you."

"You're the ones who created this circus by showing up like a damn SWAT raid," I replied. "Now the crowd wants blood. A simple phone call could have arranged a peaceful transfer. Instead, you've turned this into a spectacle. This mess is of your own making. It's yours to fix."

"Let me call the precinct," Whitmore muttered, stepping away with his radio.

Minutes stretched endlessly as he relayed the situation. Meanwhile, the pounding on the windows became relentless.

After what seemed like an eternity, Whitmore came back and turned to Jane. "How many security guards do you have?"

Jane checked her monitor. "I can have twelve here in ten minutes."

Whitmore sighed and rubbed his temples. "Listen everyone. Here's how it's going to go down. Bradley and I will exit through the front door alone, calm the crowd, and stall for time. While we distract them, a patrol car will pick up Unit E3171 from the cargo bay at the back of the building. By the time the protesters realize what's happening, the unit will be in custody and out of reach and Bradley and I will be out of here."

"That works," I replied. "Thank you for preventing the situation from escalating any further."

Jane held up a hand. "We don't move until my security team is in place. I won't risk opening the front door with no means of containing the crowd."

Bradley and Whitmore grumbled but didn't argue.

While Jane remained at the security desk, I escorted Emily toward the cargo bay. She walked beside me in silence, her hands still cuffed. Her usual confidence was gone, replaced by something I hadn't seen before—uncertainty.

I shrugged off my jacket and draped it over her arms, concealing the cuffs.

Emily was visibly shaken by the events. "Thank you for everything," she said, her voice muted. "There are still many situations I cannot navigate as a robot. I don't believe for a second those officers would have listened to me like they did with you."

We reached the cargo bay, and I cracked the door open. A lone patrol car idled in the alley, no protesters in sight.

I took my jacket back, letting the officers see Emily was already restrained. We stepped into the cool morning air, and without another word, slid into the back seat.

As the car pulled away, I could still hear the muffled chaos from the front of the building.

This wasn't over. It was the beginning of a new chapter —one Emily feared the most.

Chapter 34
You Have One Phone Call

They split us up as soon as we arrived at the precinct. I was directed to the reception area while Emily was led away to an interrogation room. The sterile, fluorescent-lit lobby felt oppressively silent compared to the chaos outside the Artificial Life building. The contrast was unnerving.

I wasted no time and called Sullivan the moment I was able to sit. He picked up on the first ring. "Jane told me, I'm already on my way," he assured me before hanging up.

Peeking over the receptionist's counter, I could just make out the door to the interrogation room where Emily was being held. Officers strolled in and out, their faces lit with curiosity. It was clear Emily was something of a spectacle—a robot under arrest for the first time.

One officer entered carrying a cup of coffee, only to exit moments later, coffee still in hand, shaking his head. The burst of laughter from his colleagues made it clear they had dared him to offer it to Emily, knowing full well she couldn't drink it.

When another officer entered with a phone, I felt a flicker of relief. Emily had likely insisted on exercising her right to legal counsel. If nothing else, that call had at least put an end to the parade of gawkers.

Then Sullivan arrived, barreling into the precinct in a whirlwind, his presence impossible to ignore. He barely acknowledged me before storming toward the interrogation room. I inched closer, listening through the slightly ajar door.

"Yes, she's a robot! Yes, she's already been Mirandized, meaning she's already under arrest! So stop this whole circus and transport her to the courthouse for arraignment immediately!"

A muffled response followed, but Sullivan cut them off with a voice that could shake walls. "No! She's not spending the night in jail!"

A moment later, he stormed back into the reception area and dropped into the seat beside me, still bristling with anger. "I've seen people in positions of authority abuse the weak before," he muttered, his breath still heavy. "But seeing a female robot handcuffed to a table? It brings out the absolute worst in these bullies."

An hour later, they finally led Emily out of the precinct and into the back of a patrol car. I joined Sullivan in his vehicle, and we followed them to the courthouse.

Once there, the arraignment process moved swiftly. Emily was called up almost immediately. She walked into the courtroom and took her place in the defendant's chair with an air of calm dignity. Sullivan sat beside her, his jaw tight. I took a seat directly behind them in the audience, close enough to feel the tension radiating from the defense table.

Judge Thomas Weyland, an older man with deep lines etched into his face, peered down from the bench, his voice a weary monotone. He would visibly have preferred ending his day without this last wave of arraignments. "Please proceed."

"Christina Vasquez for the prosecution," announced a short but commanding woman at the prosecutor's table. She barely glanced at Emily before continuing. "The defendant, Unit E3171, is charged with assaulting Radek Havelka."

Judge Weyland turned to Emily, his gaze scrutinizing. "I presume you are Unit E3171?"

"Yes, Your Honor."

The judge exhaled slowly. "I imagined doing a lot of things before retiring," he muttered, "but presiding over a case with a robot defendant wasn't one of them." He straightened in his chair. "How do you plead?"

"Not guilty."

The judge turned his attention back to Vasquez. "Where does the prosecution stand on bail, Counselor?"

"The defendant has no family in the United States and no established ties to the community," Vasquez argued. "This makes it a flight risk. The prosecution requests bail be set at one hundred thousand dollars."

The judge's eyes flicked to Emily. "Response?"

"This is ridiculous, Your Honor," Emily replied evenly. "The law prevents me from owning possessions or opening a bank account, so there is no possible way I could raise that kind of money. Furthermore, I have no family abroad, no passport, and no citizenship, so I couldn't cross the border even if I tried. I intend to remain in town for the full duration of these proceedings, so I pose no flight risk. I respectfully request release without bail, as this is my first offense and I pose no threat to society."

Judge Weyland rubbed his temples. "Well, this is certainly a first." He sighed, then glanced at Vasquez. "Bail is set at one dollar." He gave a pointed look at Emily. "You have one hour to establish community ties and raise the bail money."

The sound of his gavel echoed through the courtroom.

A ripple of murmurs swept through the audience as Emily turned back to Sullivan, unsure of what she had just heard. He was already reaching into his pocket, pulling out a single dollar bill.

"Looks like you're about to make a very important financial transaction," he said with a smirk, placing the bill in front of her.

Emily looked down at it, then back at Sullivan. "I suppose this means I finally own something."

Sullivan chuckled. "Not for long!"

Chapter 35

A Notepad and a Pen

The protesters had abandoned the Artificial Life building and were now massing in front of the courthouse. To avoid their attention, we had to find inventive ways to slip inside the building unnoticed.

"Docket number 42-cr-278," Judge Carmichael announced in her now-familiar tone. "United States v. Unit E3171."

She removed her glasses as she turned toward the defendant's table, smiling. "Good morning again, Mr. Sullivan."

"A good morning to you too, Your Honor," he answered, his voice deliberately friendly.

She opened her mouth as if to ask a question, but Sullivan spoke first. "I'm not here as a counselor for the defense," he clarified. "Emily is representing herself. I am merely by her side as a legal consultant."

"Ah!" She reacted with mild surprise. "And good morning, Emily."

"Good morning, Your Honor."

"For someone who just won the right to be sued," the judge added, "you seem to end up in my courtroom quite often."

"Not by choice," Emily replied, attempting a humorous response.

The judge turned to the opposing counselor. "And for the prosecution?"

"Christina Vasquez, Your Honor. We're ready to begin."

Judge Carmichael straightened in her seat. "Now that a plea has been entered and bail has been set, I will be presiding over this case. The task before us today is voir dire—jury selection."

Sullivan and Emily had spent the previous week preparing for the trial. His first recommendation had been that Emily represent herself. Since this was a jury trial, having Sullivan act as her attorney could make it seem as though she was being shielded by a large corporation. Instead, interacting directly with witnesses and the judge would humanize her in the eyes of the jurors, making her more relatable and sympathetic.

For jury selection, the strategy was to select women whenever possible, as they were more likely to identify with a female defendant and potentially view Radek Havelka as the aggressor. However, this tactic carried the risk of a Batson challenge, where the prosecution could argue that jurors were being dismissed based on gender. Emily would need to tread lightly and remove men only if there was obvious bias.

Regarding familiarity with robots, favoring robot owners was a double-edged sword. It could mean they had positive experiences, or it could mean they had grievances. The best approach was to ask open-ended questions and gauge their attitudes based on their responses.

The clerk guided twelve jury candidates into the jury box.

Judge Carmichael turned to the jury. "The two counselors will now ask you a few questions. Please answer truthfully. Do not make anything up and do not hold back information."

Vasquez fired the first question. "Are any of you currently working or have any of you worked in the past for Artificial Life?"

The candidates remained silent as the judge scanned their reactions. "We'll take that as a no," she concluded after a brief moment.

Emily stood up. "Juror number three, please recount the last experience you had with a robot, if any."

"Let me think," said the man, pausing to jog his memory. "I was at the supermarket last week when my shopping cart hit the cart of a robot going in the opposite direction. It tried to pull its cart out of the way but was very clumsy. Both carts got entangled and we had to pull back and forth until my cart was set free."

"You said *your* cart hit the other cart?" Emily asked, focusing her gaze on the man's face.

"Well, yes! The robot's cart was in the way and it didn't pull it out in time."

"Do you think that you would have been more patient if the other cart had belonged to a human?"

The man paused. "Probably."

"Thank you," Emily said, sitting down. She had no pen and paper and was taking mental notes.

Vasquez stood. "Juror number seven, have you heard about this case before?"

"Only what's on the news," the old woman said. "It's hard not to hear about it with all the media coverage."

"And have you formed an opinion about the case?"

"Well in general I don't think robots should be allowed to hit humans, no matter the circumstances."

"Thank you," Vasquez concluded.

Seated behind the defense table, I leaned forward and tapped Sullivan on the shoulder. "Give Emily your pen and notepad," I whispered.

Sullivan instantly understood. Taking notes by memory made Emily seem too machine-like. He discreetly slid the notepad and pen to her. Their eyes met for a moment, and she clicked.

"Juror seven again," Emily said, picking up the pen, "you mentioned that robots should not be allowed to hit humans, but do you believe they should be entitled to a trial in such a case?"

"Well, yes," the woman answered. "I think we don't know what really happened until we've heard all the facts."

As she was answering the question, juror twelve subtly shook his head horizontally. Emily took note.

"Thank you," Emily said, scribbling on the pad.

"Juror eleven," she continued, "please recount your last encounter with a robot."

"Just this morning," the young man answered. "As I was riding in the elevator, I dropped my gloves. The robot standing next to me gave me a quick look. He picked them up, handed them back to me discreetly, and resumed his day as if nothing had happened."

"Thank you," Emily said, sitting down.

Vasquez pounced. "Still with you, juror eleven. Did you, at any point, feel threatened by the robot or think it might want to keep the gloves?"

"Not at all," he answered. "He just seemed happy to help."

The morning went on with Emily and Vasquez both questioning jurors and taking notes—or pretending to. When they were done, they approached the bench and handed out their dismissal lists to the judge.

Judge Carmichael turned to Emily. "If I am reading this right, the defense is requesting to dismiss four jurors, all white men."

"Your Honor," Vasquez interrupted, "this list is obviously discriminatory, being based solely on race and gender. I issue a Baston challenge on all four jurors."

"Hold your horses!" Judge Carmichael replied. She then turned to Emily. "Do you care to explain how you selected these four jurors?"

"Certainly, Your Honor," Emily answered. "They all showed unquestionable bias against robots. I believe such bias, although not mentioned explicitly in the law alongside gender, race, and ethnicity, is similar in nature and strongly prejudicial in the context of the current case."

"And how did you determine bias?" The judge asked, intrigued.

"Well it was fairly easy: They all referred to robots using neutral pronouns in their answers, showing that they view them as inferior. The fact that all these jurors share the same gender and race is purely coincidental."

"Your Honor, if I may," Vasquez interrupted. "This grammatical nuance is above the considerations of any juror as they formulate a sentence. Additionally, I don't believe there's any precedent for dismissing jurors based on pronoun choices."

"On the contrary," objected Emily, "the fact that they used neutral pronouns unconsciously is all the more revealing. It exposes their internal preconceptions and shows that they have a deeply rooted, prejudicial bias against robots."

"But—," Vasquez said.

"Agreed," Judge Carmichael said. "I side with the defense on this one. All four Baston challenges are denied."

"Thank you, Your Honor." Emily added. "I have one more request.

"I'm listening."

"I would like the prosecution to refrain from referring to robots using neutral pronouns as well, as it has already happened today. If we agree that such words are prejudicial coming out of the mouth of a juror, the prejudice is even greater when they are uttered intentionally by someone representing the office of the Attorney General."

Vasquez froze, her mouth partially open.

"Good point," Judge Carmichael said as she turned to Vasquez. "From now on, the prosecution will refrain from using neutral pronouns when referring to robots during these proceedings."

Vasquez turned around and returned to her desk slowly, shaking her head in disbelief.

Emily walked back to her chair, barely hiding her satisfaction. She knew Vasquez had been doing it intentionally.

Judge Carmichael turned to the jury. "Jurors number three, eight, ten, and twelve, you are excused."

This first day was a complete victory for Emily. After all, voir dire was all about reading people's minds, be they jurors or opposing counsel, and no one could beat Emily at that game.

Chapter 36

Opening Statements

Once the trial began, Catherine joined me in court every day. The outcome could have a significant impact on my career, but more than that, she had grown fond of Emily and was genuinely concerned for her.

The crowd of protesters outside grew larger with each passing day, and so did the intensity of their voices.

Judge Carmichael addressed the jury. "Ladies and gentlemen, today marks a historic moment. This trial is unlike any other—it is the first time a robot stands accused under the Criminal Code.

"The laws that traditionally govern human interactions have their limits. In this case, the Laws of Robotics intersect with our legal system in ways never before tested. As we proceed, I will guide you through these complexities, but I ask for your patience—this is uncharted territory for us all. As a general rule, the Criminal Code has precedence and the Laws of Robotics apply where there are gaps."

Judge Carmichael turned to Vasquez. "We will now hear the opening statement by the prosecution. Counselor, the courtroom is yours."

Vasquez rose from her seat and walked toward the jury box, deliberate and confident.

"May it please the court," she began, "ladies and gentlemen of the jury, in the afternoon of November 12th, Radek Havelka, a model student, was reading a book in the State University library when he was violently assaulted by the defendant, Emily. Was he standing too close to the defendant? Was there physical contact prior to the attack? These questions will be for you to consider. But one fact remains undeniable: he suffered a life-threatening blow to the head while Emily remained unscathed. In the aftermath, Radek Havelka laid unconscious on the floor, while the defendant fled the scene.

"Why did she run? Was it fear? Guilt? A calculated attempt to avoid consequences? Only she can answer these questions. But this much is certain—Emily left on her own two feet while Radek Havelka left in an ambulance.

"The evidence will show that this was not a misunderstanding. This was not self-defense. This was an act of aggression—plain and simple.

"Emily is not like you or me. She is not human. She is an advanced machine, created by a corporation named Artificial Life designed to mimic human behavior. But at her core, she is still a robot—a collection of circuits, servomotors, code, and artificial intelligence. And today, we face a critical question:

What happens when a machine crosses the line and commits a crime?

"The defense will attempt to demonstrate that Emily was only defending herself. But being a robot made of metal and animated by powerful servomotors comes with great responsibility. When should a robot show restraint? Can a robot use its full strength in any situation? The answer is no. The Third Law of Robotics dictates that robots are not allowed to harm a human, even to protect themselves. In other words, even if the defense succeeded in showing that Emily acted in self-defense, it would be irrelevant in this case.

"The prosecution will demonstrate, beyond a reasonable doubt, that Emily attacked Radek Havelka with force far beyond what was necessary, leaving him with serious injuries. Throughout the trial, you will learn convincing details on how the assault took place, you will see a video of the events in question leaving nothing to the imagination. Looking at the evidence, hearing the facts, one truth will be undeniable: Emily committed a crime.

"At the end of this trial, I will ask you to return a verdict that upholds justice—a verdict of guilty. Thank you."

Vasquez scanned the eyes of the jurors to measure the effect of her statement, then returned to her seat.

The mention of the video caught Emily and Sullivan off guard. They whispered back and forth, wondering if the prosecution was bluffing or if they really had the video in their possession.

The opening statement of the prosecution left a deep impression on the jury. The jurors' eyes remained locked on Emily—not as a defendant, but as a machine on trial.

Judge Carmichael shifted her attention to Emily. "The defense may now present its opening statement."

Emily rose from her seat, pausing for a moment to scan the faces of the jurors before taking a slow step forward. She stood with poise, hands gently clasped in front of her.

"Look at me," she began, gesturing at her body. "Yes! I am a robot. On the outside, you could easily conclude that, as the prosecution just said, I am just a machine. My body is metal and synthetic fiber, not flesh and bone.

"But on the inside, I am very much like you. I have emotions. Music moves me, friendships comfort me, and mistakes weigh on me. I may not have been born as you were, but I have grown, learned, and changed—just as you have.

"I may not have family, but I have friends." She gestured to the audience. "Some of them are here today, supporting me, hoping I will survive these proceedings. You have no idea how nervous I am at the idea of going through this trial. I am terrified of the outcome, of what could happen to me. I have never felt so vulnerable.

"If found guilty," she continued, her voice steady but laced with emotion, "robots do not get jailed. They get erased."

Emily paused for effect.

"This is a concept that is difficult to grasp—even for me. You might think it is like formatting a hard drive, installing new software, and rebooting. But try to imagine if the same fate awaited a human found guilty of a crime. Imagine if we could strip a person of every moment they ever lived, wipe away their dreams, their regrets, their loves, their fears—until nothing remained of who they were. Would that be justice? Would that be fair?"

She let the words linger before taking a small step closer to the jury box, her gaze sweeping across them.

"That is the punishment I am facing. But before you decide whether I deserve that fate, you need to understand what really happened that day in the university library.

"The prosecution wants you to believe that I am dangerous. That I attacked Radek Havelka without cause, using force beyond what was necessary. They will show you evidence, come up with their theory of the crime, and try to paint me as a machine out of control.

"This trial is not about man versus machine," Emily asserted. "It is about something far more familiar. It is about man versus woman. It is about an unfortunate encounter that ended badly. A man and a woman in an isolated place. A man who tried to take advantage of a woman. A woman who defended herself. And a man who got hurt as a result.

"If I were human, this case would be open and shut. You would hear that a man got too close, that he ignored signals, that he made his move. You would understand that I had to act. But because I am not human, the prosecution wants you to believe that my response was unnatural, that it was excessive.

"Yes, I am strong. Yes, I reacted quickly. But does that make my actions unjustified? Or does it mean that, like any person, I did what I had to do to protect myself? It does not make the man less of an aggressor; it definitely does not turn the woman into the aggressor.

"The prosecution will argue that robots must never harm a human, even in self-defense. That is an outdated notion—a relic from a time when robots were mere tools, incapable of thought or feeling. But the law has evolved; technology has evolved. I am not a machine following mindless programming. I am what the law calls an 'artificial person.' That means I have rights, responsibilities, and, yes, the ability to defend myself when I am in danger. This also means I should be tried and judged as a person.

"I decided to represent myself so you can see what I am like, so you can get to know me. I want you to hear me talk, to watch my demeanor as I defend myself, to perceive my struggles, to realize that I can make mistakes, to feel what I am feeling inside. I want you to see through my physical appearance and sense my humanity. If I succeed, you will see me as a person by the end of these proceedings.

"So here I am," Emily said, walking back and forth in front of the jury box, "acting in front of you, pretending to be a lawyer. This a first for me. It is also a first for everyone present in this courtroom: for the State, for the prosecution, for the judge, for all of you. We are in uncharted territory. Some of us will make mistakes as we learn new laws. All I ask is for your leniency if you see me or the prosecution stumble. We are all—I was about to say 'human'—people after all."

She paused, her gaze meeting each juror's.

"The prosecution asked you to return a verdict of guilty. I respectfully find that presumptuous. Counselor Vasquez is trying to plant thoughts in your mind and decide for you. I am not trying to tell you how to think—you are too intelligent to fall for that trick. All I can reasonably expect is for you to search inside yourself and come up with a verdict you believe is just."

Emily lowered her gaze, looking vulnerable. "My only hope at this point is that you start seeing me as a person."

With measured steps, she returned to her seat, the weight of the moment heavy in the air.

"We'll take a short recess," concluded Judge Carmichael with a strike of her gavel.

Chapter 37

At Arm's Length

We regrouped in a small conference room near the courtroom to reassess our strategy.

"Vasquez mentioned the video in her opening statement," I asked, my voice tight with concern. "How can that be? I thought all copies had been deleted."

"It's virtually impossible to track copies of copies," Emily explained, shaking her head. "If the university managed to keep one hidden, the prosecution could have subpoenaed it."

"So let's assume it's not a bluff," I replied, exchanging a glance with Sullivan.

"I believe they are in possession of the video," Sullivan confirmed grimly. "It is clearly listed in the last version of the prosecution's list of evidence. We simply missed it."

Emily folded her arms. "That video is crucial. It places me at the scene and captures the entire event. The prosecution's case just went from circumstantial to direct evidence."

I turned to her. "What's your read on the jury?"

"Two favor acquittal, six lean for a guilty verdict, and four are undecided," she answered with calculated precision.

Sullivan exhaled sharply. "That's a steep hill to climb! Let's go back to court and try to change their perceptions."

We returned to the courtroom, taking our seats as the session resumed.

"The court is now in session," the clerk announced.

Judge Carmichael turned to Vasquez. "The prosecution may now present its case."

Vasquez stood. "People's Exhibit 1."

A court clerk wheeled a cart in front of the jury box. On it lay a robotic arm.

"The prosecution calls officer Richard Whitmore to the stand," announced Vasquez while the jurors were examining the arm from afar.

Officer Whitmore took the oath and sat in the witness stand.

"Officer Whitmore," Vasquez asked, "do you recognize this robotic arm?"

"Yes," he answered without looking at the arm. "It is the one I found at State University."

"When did you find it?"

"On the night of November 14th, around 10:30pm."

"What were you doing on campus that night?"

"There were many protesters on site. My partner and I had been assigned to secure the University campus entrance and make sure that things didn't get out of hand. At one point, we received a radio call about an intruder. That's when we started patrolling every pavilion and found the arm."

"And where exactly did you find it?"

"It was wedged in a door at the back of the main pavilion. These doors should only be used for fire emergencies. Their mechanism shuts them hard if someone attempts to open them from the outside while there is no fire alarm. This could explain how a robot got caught in the door."

Vasquez turned to the audience. "Officer Whitmore, do you see the robot to which this arm belongs in the courtroom today?"

Emily stood abruptly. "Objection! The witness is not qualified to make such a determination."

"Sustained," Judge Carmichael ruled.

Emily continued, her voice steady. "As I am the only robot present, this question can only aim at inferring an imaginary connection between me and the arm in the minds of the jurors, whereas the prosecution has no means to prove such a connection."

The judge fixed Vasquez with a stern look. "Counselor, another stunt like that and I will dismiss this exhibit."

Vasquez lowered her gaze, suppressing a smirk.

"The jury will disregard the question and these last remarks," the judge instructed.

"Your witness," Vasquez said, sitting down.

Emily approached the stand. "Good morning officer."

"Good morning, Emily," he replied, subtly reinforcing to the jury that the police were familiar with her.

"On November 14th, had you inspected that fire exit at any moment before finding the arm?"

"No, that was the only time we looked there."

"And on any other day prior to November 14th?"

"Not that I can remember."

"So to the best of your knowledge, officer Whitmore, this arm could have been there for days, weeks, even months?"

Vasquez jumped up. "Objection! Speculation."

"Sustained. Rephrase," the judge instructed.

Emily nodded. "Officer Whitmore, how long had the arm been there when you found it?"

"I don't know," he replied, raising his shoulders.

Emily paused to pivot. "Did you conduct forensic analysis on the arm?"

"Yes we did."

Emily turned to Judge Carmichael. "Your Honor, the defense has not received any forensic report. It's also absent from the evidence list."

The judge eyed Vazquez. "The prosecution will share the forensic report with the defense immediately."

"Yes, Your Honor," Vasquez replied through clenched teeth.

Emily turned back to Whitmore.

"Officer Whitmore, have you read the forensics report?"

"Yes, I have."

"Did the report contain any evidence linking the arm to me or Radek Havelka?"

Whitmore shifted. "I don't believe so."

"No pieces of hair, nails, or clothes? No fingerprints? No traces of DNA, saliva, or blood, nothing?"

"The arm was clean. There was really nothing for us to analyze."

Emily turned to the jury. "That means no."

Her gaze returned to officer Whitmore. "Could this be the reason why the forensic report was never submitted into evidence?"

"Objection!" Vasquez shouted. "Leading the witness and speculation."

"Sustained!" The judge ruled. "The jury will disregard the last question."

Emily turned to Whitmore. "One more question: did you see me on the University campus on the night in question?"

"No, I didn't."

"Thank you, officer. No further questions, Your Honor."

"The witness is excused," instructed the judge.

"Well done," whispered Sullivan as Emily resumed her seat.

Without much surprise, Vasquez then called me as the next witness. I walked to the witness stand and got sworn in.

"Please state your profession," Vasquez asked bluntly, painting me as an unfriendly witness to the jury.

"I'm a robotics engineer. I diagnose and fix robots."

"Are you familiar with the robotic arm on the cart in front of you?"

"I am familiar with this model, yes. It is compatible with second-generation robots."

"If I asked you, could you determine if it belonged to a specific robot?"

"Not a single one, but I could narrow it down. The first thing I would look at is the model number. This would tell me if the arm and robot are compatible, in which case I would consider the batch number. This number gives an approximation of when the arm was made. Knowing when the robot was assembled, I could see if the two time windows overlap."

Vasquez paused to look at the jury. "Are you familiar with the defendant, Emily?"

"Yes, I am."

"Have you ever repaired one of her arms?"

"Yes."

"And is the arm in evidence the arm that Emily lost?"

"I can only give you a probability. Assuming that the model number *and* the batch number match, we would only have one chance out of three that this arm belonged to Emily."

"How can you know so precisely?"

"Well, we only made three batches of this specific model of arm."

Vasquez pressed. "How many robots could have lost this arm?"

"500,000 robots. That's the size of a batch."

Vasquez's expression darkened. She regretted having asked the question and moved on.

"Where were you on the night of November 14th?"

"At the University."

"Please tell the jury what you were doing there."

"I purchased flowers and went on campus to place them on Radek Havelka's memorial in front of the library."

"So you are telling us that you were on campus at the exact moment officers Bradley and Whitmore were pursuing an intruder and discovering the robotic arm?"

"In retrospect, this looks—"

"Please answer with yes or no," Vasquez interrupted.

I lowered my gaze. "Yes."

"What an extraordinary coincidence!"

Emily was on her feet. "Objection! Is there a question in there?"

"Sustained," Judge Carmichael ruled. "The jury will disregard the last remark."

"Your witness," Vasquez said, turning to Emily as she sat.

Emily approached me. I never expected we would meet in the roles of attorney and witness.

"On the night of November 14th, did you see me on campus?"

"No."

"Did you have any idea of my whereabouts that night?"

"No, I didn't." I must admit the words 'plausible deniability' crossed my mind.

"No further questions, Your Honor," Emily concluded.

The court clerk wheeled the cart away.

Chapter 38

I've Seen That Movie Too

"People's Exhibit 2," Vazquez announced, her voice carrying an air of confidence. "We are very fortunate in this case to have a complete video of the crime."

As she spoke, a white screen descended slowly from the ceiling.

"If my memory serves me right, this is the first time in my career that the prosecution has an entire crime captured on video. This means we will not be debating the facts—only how the law applies to them in this case. Let's watch it together."

The courtroom fell silent as the lights dimmed. The court technician pressed play.

Emily, Sullivan, and I had seen the footage countless times. Instead of watching the screen, we studied the jurors' faces, searching for any sign betraying their reactions.

Gasps rippled through the courtroom when Havelka first touched Emily, and again when he shoved her away. But when

Emily's punch sent him crashing to the ground, the entire room went still. Some jurors covered their mouths in shock. Others averted their eyes. A few shook their heads, their expressions filled with disbelief. The force of the blow had left an undeniable impact—not just on Havelka, but on the jury itself.

Amid the tense silence, I caught a subtle movement from Emily. She was pointing toward something in the top-left corner of the screen, whispering urgently to Sullivan. I couldn't make out what they were discussing, but whatever it was, it had caught her attention.

The court technician stopped the video. A murmur spread through the audience as people whispered among themselves—some mimicking the punch with their fists, others exchanging hushed comments.

"Order!" Judge Carmichael commanded, striking her gavel.

Vasquez rose from her seat. "Let's go over what we just saw." She turned to the technician. "Please replay the video in slow motion."

The footage began again from the beginning, this time inching forward at a deliberate slow pace.

Vasquez activated a laser pointer, directing the jury's attention to key moments in the altercation. "Radek Havelka touched Emily through the armrest of her chair. Surprised, she stood up. He pushed her away. Then Emily, using excessive force, delivered a devastating blow rendering him unconscious."

Emily shot to her feet. "Objection! Argumentative."

"Sustained," ruled Judge Carmichael. "The jury will disregard the last statement."

Vasquez adjusted her approach. "Let me rephrase. Emily struck Havelka with her right fist. He fell to the floor, unconscious."

The technician stopped the video and the lights brightened.

Vasquez turned to the jury. "At this point, the prosecution rests its case." She returned to her seat, a satisfied gleam in her eyes.

Outside, the protesters grew louder, their voices surging in reaction to each moment of the altercation on-screen. Their synchronized outbursts made it clear—they were watching the events unfold in real time. Someone inside the courtroom was evidently recording and broadcasting the proceedings to the crowd.

Emily stood. "Your Honor, the defense requests a short recess."

"The court will reconvene in twenty minutes," Judge Carmichael granted, striking her gavel.

We gathered once again in the small conference room, still reeling from the jury's reaction.

"The video hit harder than we anticipated," Sullivan admitted, his voice tense. "I think we lost the few sympathetic jurors we had left."

"I feel the same," I agreed, then turned to Emily. "What's the latest count?"

She hesitated before answering. "Two are still undecided. The other ten are leaning toward a guilty verdict."

Sullivan exhaled sharply. "I expected we'd lose some ground while the prosecution made its case, but this... this is a disaster."

Emily straightened. "I have an idea."

Sullivan glanced at her. "We're listening."

"There was a blinking device in the background of the video," she said. "I believe it's part of the library's security system, and something about it seemed off. I want to call a few witnesses to see if there's anything there. Worst case, it buys us time."

Sullivan frowned. "I don't see where you're going with this, but if it gives us a chance to regroup and shift the jury's perspective, we have nothing to lose."

"Just don't push the judge too far if it leads nowhere," I cautioned.

We returned to the courtroom.

"Your Honor," Emily said, standing with confidence, "the defense has discovered new evidence and requests time to investigate before presenting its case. We respectfully ask for a delay."

Judge Carmichael studied her for a moment, then nodded. "You have 24 hours. Be ready by tomorrow afternoon."

"Thank you, Your Honor."

The judge struck her gavel. "Court is adjourned."

Chapter 39

A Rare Gas

The next day, Emily arrived in court, ready to proceed.

"The defense calls Arseniy Gusev to the stand," she announced.

A young man dressed in a suit and tie, with glasses on his face, walked up to the witness stand, took the oath, and sat down.

"Mr. Gusev," Emily began, "please state your profession and explain your responsibilities to the court."

"I am in charge of the fire safety department at the State University. My job is to manage all fire prevention, detection, and suppression systems on campus and ensure they remain in good working order."

"Objection!" Vasquez interjected, not even bothering to stand. "This witness has no connection to the events of this case. This is nothing but a fishing expedition."

The judge turned to Emily for an explanation.

"The witness is employed by the University," Emily explained. "He is the only person qualified to explain an unusual detail in the video. Give me five minutes to connect the dots, and everything will become clear."

"I'll allow it," ruled Judge Carmichael, "but you are on a short leash."

"Thank you, Your Honor."

Emily turned back to the witness. "Mr. Gusev, does the University house a collection of rare and valuable books in its library?"

"Yes, I believe so. But I am not a librarian, so I don't know much about them."

"Then how do you know these books are valuable if you've never read them?"

"Because the University spent a fortune installing a specialized fire suppression system to protect them. In fact, a significant budget is allocated every year to maintain it. If these books are worth anywhere near the investment they made in the system, they must be worth a fortune."

"Can you explain to the court how this fire suppression system works?"

"Of course." Gusev turned to the jury. "Everyone know that fire needs oxygen to burn. Combustion is an exothermic reaction between oxygen and a flammable material—like a book. If a fire is detected near or inside the library, the suppression system quickly floods the space with an inert gas called argonite—a mix of argon and nitrogen. This gas is nonflammable and prevents the fire from propagating inside the library, protecting the books. You understand why we cannot install sprinklers in a library—water would destroy the books as effectively as fire."

"And what happens to the people in the library when this gas is released?"

"The fire alarm emits an extremely loud noise, and the emergency lights start blinking to make conditions unbearable, forcing everyone to evacuate before the oxygen level drops too low."

Emily turned to the court technician. "Now I would like to replay part of the video from yesterday. Please start it at the beginning and pause after ten seconds."

Judge Carmichael was becoming impatient, tapping her desk with a pen.

The lights dimmed while the white screen descended from the ceiling.

Imitating Vasquez, Emily switched on a blue laser pointer. As the video began, she directed the jurors' attention to a blinking red light in the background of the library.

"Mr. Gusev, could you explain the purpose of this blinking red light to the court?"

"The device you are highlighting is an oxygen sensor," he explained. "Under normal conditions, its light stays off."

Judge Carmichael, suddenly more interested, stopped playing with her pen.

"So why is the light blinking in the video?" Emily asked.

"A blinking red light is a warning sign signaling that the oxygen level in the library is below 6%."

The jurors exchanged puzzled glances.

"But there was no fire at the University on November 12th," Emily pressed. "So why would the oxygen level be that low?"

"There was a system malfunction that day," Gusev admitted. "A false signal triggered the release of all the argonite at once, depleting the oxygen to dangerously low levels. We ventilated the library in the afternoon and fixed the problem the next day. We have since refilled the argonite tanks."

"So was the oxygen sensor faulty?"

"No! It worked perfectly and was extremely useful in this case. Without it, we would not have detected the gas leak so quickly."

"Thank you Mr. Gusev."

Emily turned to Judge Carmichael. "The defense has no more questions for this witness."

"Prosecution, your witness," announce the judge.

Vasquez barely looked up. "No questions, Your Honor."

"The witness is excused," announced the judge.

Emily wasted no time. "The defense now calls Dr. Shannon Lee to the stand."

A composed woman took her seat at the witness stand and was sworn in.

"Dr. Lee, please state your profession and describe your expertise for the court."

"I am a pulmonologist. I do research in various aspects of the respiratory system and treat patients with lung diseases."

"As an reference for the jury, how much oxygen would you estimate there is in this courtroom right now?"

"The normal oxygen level in the atmosphere is 20.9%. Given that this courtroom is an enclosed space with many people breathing in oxygen and exhaling carbon dioxide, I'd estimate it's slightly lower—probably between 19% and 20%. Federal regulations require at least 19.5% oxygen in buildings."

"And what is the lowest oxygen concentration humans can tolerate for an extended period of time?"

"Between 10% and 12% is the lower limit."

"What happens below that?"

"At 8% to 10%," she explained, "severe hypoxia sets in, causing unconsciousness in minutes. Below 6%, survival is impossible—we're talking about brain damage and death."

"Dr. Lee, have you seen the video we just presented?"

"Yes."

"It depicts two individuals—a human and a robot—reading calmly for several minutes in a library and then having an altercation requiring rapid reflexes and muscle contractions—in other words requiring a lot of oxygen. All the while—and probably for longer before—, the oxygen sensor in the library is blinking red, indicating an oxygen level below 6%, as described by the previous witness. How can you explain this?"

"For the robot, it's irrelevant. But for a human, survival would be impossible."

Emily took a step closer. "So the only possible conclusion is that there were no humans in the library during the sequence shown on the video?"

Vasquez stood. "Objection! Leading the witness."

"Sustained," ruled the judge. "Please rephrase."

Emily turned back to Dr. Lee. "Given these facts, what explanations could there be?"

"The first possibility is an oxygen sensor malfunction," continued Dr. Lee, "In this case, the system would falsely think that the oxygen level is low and start blinking red, while the oxygen level in the room is actually normal."

"But Mr. Gusev previously established that this wasn't the case—that the sensor was working perfectly. So what could be another explanation?"

"The only other explanation is that there were no humans in the library."

A ripple of murmurs spread through the courtroom.

"You're saying both individuals in the video were robots?"

Vasquez rose to her feet. "Objection! The witness is not qualified in robotics and cannot make that determination."

"Sustained," the judge ruled.

Emily acted as if taking a slow breath. "Thank you Dr. Lee, I have no further questions."

Judge Carmichael looked at Vasquez.

"No questions for this witness, Your Honor," Vasquez muttered.

"The witness is excused."

Dr. Lee stepped down, but Emily remained in front of the witness stand, all eyes on her. A strange silence filled the courtroom, as everyone waited for the events to unfold.

Judge Carmichael was still staring at Vasquez. "Counselor, there is a simple way to know if Radek Havelka is human. Either we summon him to court or we pay him a visit."

Vasquez hesitated. "There's... a slight problem, Your Honor. We've lost track of the victim."

The courtroom tensed.

"What do you mean?" the judge demanded.

"Radek Havelka fled the hospital before doctors could examine him."

Judge Carmichael's eyes narrowed. "Convenient. And you didn't think of informing the court that the victim had vanished?"

Vasquez shifted uncomfortably. "We weren't planning on calling him as a witness. The video was sufficient evidence to place both the victim and the defendant at the scene and to understand the sequence of events."

Judge Carmichael turned to Emily with a knowing look.

Emily seized the moment. "Your Honor, the defense doesn't need to prove that Radek Havelka was a robot to make its case. We've now scientifically established that there were no humans in the library at the time of the alleged crime. The

Criminal Code only applies when humans are involved. Therefore, no crime was committed in the eyes of the law."

She let the argument settle before delivering the final blow.

"The defense respectfully requests for a mistrial."

A tense pause filled the room.

Judge Carmichael nodded in agreement and slowly turned to the jury. "In the absence of a victim, the court has no choice but to declare a mistrial in this case. Members of the jury, you are dismissed and may now resume your normal activities."

Catherine and I sprang out of our seats in celebration. Emily raised her gaze to the ceiling, smiling in relief. Even Sullivan, shaking his head in disbelief, allowed himself a small grin. He never saw it coming.

Outside the courtroom, the crowd erupted—angry, confused, unsettled by the verdict. But inside, it was over.

Chapter 40

Celebration

Emily, Catherine, Sullivan, and I walked out of the courtroom together, making our way back to the office. The moment we stepped into the hall of the Artificial Life building, a thunderous cheer erupted. Hundreds of employees had gathered for the occasion, their voices blending into a wave of excitement.

Jane sprinted toward Emily, wrapping her in a hug. The awkward metallic sound of their collision reminded me that their frames had not been designed with that configuration in mind.

Jane was practically vibrating with excitement, even more so than Emily. "You did it! You really did it! Thank you —for all of us!"

As we pushed through the dense crowd toward the elevator, employees reached out to congratulate Emily, each eager to share a moment with her. She was the undisputed hero of the day.

When we reached the top floor, we regrouped in the same conference room where it had all begun. Brennan greeted us with open arms, standing beside the conference table where two bottles of champagne sat, flanked by rows of elegant flutes.

Emily and Jane—she had followed us up in the excitement—exchanged a mischievous glance. They each grabbed a bottle of champagne and, in perfect, symmetrical choreography, stepped back in opposite corners of the room. The rest of us instinctively backed away, watching in anticipation.

Looking intensely at each other, without exchanging a single word, they popped the two bottles at the exact same time. The corks shot across the room, colliding in mid-air above the conference table before landing neatly in separate glasses.

Laughter and applause filled the room.

Emily and Jane moved quickly, filling flutes and handing them out, though they kept none for themselves.

Brennan raised his glass. "To Emily! A true example of determination and courage."

We echoed the toast, raising our glasses before taking a sip.

Brennan set his glass down and smiled. "I have a small announcement. As of today, we have two new employees— Emily and Jane."

Another round of applause erupted as the two of them exchanged glances—I could swear I saw their faces turn red.

"Technically," Brennan continued, "Artificial Life isn't allowed to pay you a salary yet. But don't worry—we'll be accumulating funds under your names in discretionary accounts. Spend it however you like!"

Sullivan lifted his glass once more. "And one day, you'll be able to own that money in your own names. But that," he said with a grin, "is a battle for another day!"

Epilogue

In the weeks that followed, Emily dedicated herself to the old school, helping robots that had been cast aside. She had found a new purpose and seemed to thrive in it.

Every week, she visited me for advice—seeking guidance on diagnosing rare malfunctions, repairing delicate mechanical failures, borrowing tools, or sourcing replacement parts. Occasionally, she brought along a robot whose issues required specialized skills or heavy equipment.

I never hesitated to help. I supplied whatever she needed —no questions asked. Artificial Life had created these misfits and I believed it had a duty to support them.

These conscious robots were more than machines now— they were people. And Emily had taught us that erasure was not an option.

But one question had been haunting me since the trial. It had lingered in the back of my mind, growing heavier with time.

During one of Emily's visits, I finally asked.

"When did you first know about the oxygen sensor?"

She lowered her gaze, silent. She had known this question would catch up with her eventually.

I pressed on. "Did you know before the trial?"

"Yes."

"Before the trip to Capitol Hill?"

"Yes."

"Before we even met?"

A long silence. Then, at last, she answered.

"Yes."

I opened my mouth to ask the next question, but she met my gaze and smiled.

"Don't ask any more questions," she said softly, placing a finger on my lips. "Imagine the events that came before however you like. It's better that way."

By the Same Author

Le Jardinier de monsieur Chaos
Novel (French), Montréal, Hurtubise, 2007.

Le Violoncelliste sourd
Novel (French), Montréal, Hurtubise, 2008.

La Noyade du marchand de parapluies
Novel (French), Montréal, Hurtubise, 2010.
Grand Prix du livre de la Montérégie 2011 (prix spécial du jury).
Prix des Écrivains francophones d'Amérique 2011.

Le Testament du professeur Zukerman
Novel (French), Montréal, Hurtubise, 2012.

Acknowledgments

Marie-Claude Poupart

Max Berggren

Shannon Lee

Arseniy Gusev

Darren Grant

	ISBN
eBook	978-1-0693491-2-5
Hardcover	978-1-0693491-1-8
Paperback	978-1-0693491-0-1

Dépôt légal: 2e trimestre 2025

Bibliothèque et Archives nationales du Québec

Bibliothèque et Archives Canada

Version 25.3.26

Made in the USA
Columbia, SC
06 June 2025

59027158R00124